*A
Harlequin
Romance*

OTHER
Harlequin Romances
by RUTH CLEMENCE

1195—SPREAD YOUR WINGS
 (Originally published under the title 'A North Country Lass')
1418—A CURE WITH KINDNESS
1619—HAPPY WITH EITHER

THE MAN
FROM
RHODESIA

by

RUTH CLEMENCE

HARLEQUIN BOOKS   TORONTO
WINNIPEG

First published in 1966 by Mills & Boon Limited,
50 Grafton Way, Fitzroy Square, London, England.

Harlequin edition published
November, 1966

Reprinted 1973

Printed in Canada

CHAPTER ONE

As Margaret Grant walked up the steps of the house in Chester Square and put her key into the lock, she thought for perhaps the hundredth time how fortunate she had been to find this job. When Mrs. Grant had had a stroke nearly three years ago, things had seemed very black. Margaret had given up her job with an engineering firm in order to nurse her mother, and by the time Mrs. Grant was convalescing, Margaret realized she would not be able to take another full-time job.

The stroke had left Mrs. Grant with a paralysed left hand and arm, and Margaret began to look around for employment which would enable her to attend to her mother's toilet in the mornings, and to arrive home at the latest by mid-afternoon. On her first visit to the employment agency, when she had stated her requirements they had shaken their heads. She was told that hopes of getting a job of this description were remote and in any case would be poorly paid. Then, after three weeks, the agency had telephoned her one morning to tell her they had an inquiry they thought might interest her. A client wanted a companion/secretary, but the hours were to be from ten-thirty in the morning, until four p.m. The applicant must be an adaptable person, willing to fit in with the household, but on the other hand, the salary offered was surprisingly generous. Margaret had not hesitated. She was willing to try anything which would enable her, not only to earn a living, but also to look after her mother as much as possible, and this offer seemed like a gift from heaven.

As she closed the front door and walked across the

wide hall to her small office, Margaret thought about her first day here. On that morning she had been admitted to the house by a tall, gaunt woman who had introduced herself as "Nannie Macgennis". She had been taken into the small room at the rear of the house which had been converted into an office. Mrs. Macgennis had shown her where to hang her hat and coat, explained the indoor telephone which she said had recently been installed, and then had gone upstairs to tell Mrs. Hollis that Margaret had arrived. Margaret had only met her employer for a brief interview a fortnight previously, and so far had formed only an agreeable impression of a vague, diminutive lady, with a riot of grey curls and very beautiful smoke-grey eyes.

She was soon to discover that the vague air was deceptive and that it masked a shrewd brain. Alicia Hollis was Irish by birth, the widow of a wealthy business man who had, in later life, devoted his time to charitable enterprises. On his death, his wife had not only carried on his wishes in this respect, but had made it her business to interest others. She was a member of a great many charitable committees, and when she took over the post, Margaret discovered that her hours were very fully occupied.

It had not taken her long to discover why the agency had been asked to find an adaptable person. Not only did she attend to all Mrs. Hollis's correspondence, personal as well as for her charities, but she soon found that most of the household business fell on her shoulders. She kept the accounts, paid the wages, had the ordering of everything, from groceries to new curtains and bed linen, sent for workmen when this became necessary and even did the cooking one never-to-be-forgotten week when Mrs. Macgennis and the cook had gone down with 'flu.

Now, nearly three years later, Margaret couldn't imagine working anywhere else. Always a generous and considerate employer, Mrs. Hollis treated her almost like a daughter, and from time to time, to Margaret's intense embarrassment, had been heard to refer to her as "my good right hand".

As she was starting to open the mail this particular morning, there was a gentle knock and the door opened. Mrs. Macgennis came in carrying a small tray of coffee and biscuits. As ever, she was dressed in an old- fashioned black dress with a small white lace collar high to the neck. Speaking in her pronounced brouge, she said, "Tis a beautiful morning, O'im thinkin'."

"It is, indeed, Mrs. Macgennis," Margaret replied. She cleared a space on the desk for the tray. As she did so she looked up and smiled. Mrs. Macgennis was Mrs. Hollis's old nannie. She had come over from Ireland on her mistress's marriage, nannied the two sons after they were born, and was now something of an institution in the house. She must have been in her middle seventies, or even more, but she was still very upright, and harried everyone in the household from Mrs. Hollis herself down to the daily woman. Ever since Margaret had come to work there, Mrs. Macgennis had carried in coffee for her on her arrival, and she invariably stopped for a few minutes gossip.

Her favourite topic was the Hollis family itself. Mrs. Hollis had two sons. The elder, Nicholas, lived in Rhodesia. Margaret had never met him as he had returned to Africa after a long visit home just before she had started her job nearly three years previously. He had not been back since. The younger son, Miles, was a research doctor. He lived at home and Margaret thought he must be the living image of everyone's idea of an absent-minded professor. Sometimes, Dr. Miles, as Nannie Macgennis always called him, used to wander into the office and ask Margaret to do some typing for him, looking as if he hardly knew whether he was at home or in his laboratory at the hospital. Margaret

7

knew from Mrs. Macgennis that Miles Hollis was only thirty-three, but he looked years older and was already nearly bald.

As she drank her coffee, Margaret finished opening and sorting the morning mail. She read each letter as she opened it, afterwards putting them in neat piles. Some she could answer herself without any trouble. Some required Mrs. Hollis's personal attention, while others were of a doubtful nature and would require some thought. As she opened the last envelope the house telephone rang. Mrs. Hollis spoke requesting Margaret to come up to her sitting-room.

Margaret picked up her pad, pencils and the piles of letters and went out into the hall. The house was a good deal larger than it appeared from the outside. On one side of the ground floor hall, in addition to her own office there was a dining-room and a cloakroom. On the opposite side was the library and the entrance to the kitchen and a diminutive garden.

As she walked upstairs, Margaret admired once again the thick moss-green carpeting, and the sheen of the polished balustrade. She knocked at a door at the head of the stairs, and Mrs. Hollis called to her to come in.

"Good morning, my dear. Is there a great deal this morning?"

"Yes," Margaret replied. "It was quite a heavy post today."

Without wasting any time on idle conversation, they plunged into a discussion of the various household matters requiring attention and then dealt with the letters, It was lunchtime before Mrs. Hollis was satisfied that she had solved all the day's problems. As Margaret was opening the door she suddenly asked, "How is your mother today?"

"About the same, thank you," Margaret answered, "though she does seem to have improved since her treatment with the new physiotherapy the doctor suggested."

In her own office, she put her papers carefully on the desk before going to wash her hands. Then she went along to the kitchen and after a few words with Cook carried her lunch tray back to the office. She put it down on the small table in the window. Unwrapping her table-napkin, she sat gazing out at the sunshine in the small garden outside. At this time of the year there was not much to look at. The few flowers which Mrs. Hollis persuaded to grow were over, and the climber roses hung down from the trellis pleading to be pruned and tied back. Margaret, as she ate her lunch, promised herself half an hour's work out there when time permitted.

After a short rest, Margaret sat down at the typewriter and worked steadily through the morning's correspondence. The pile of neatly typed letters at her side gradually mounted, and at a quarter to four she carried those requiring signature upstairs. She knocked at the sitting-room door, but there was no answer, so leaving the letters on Mrs. Hollis's desk, she returned downstairs to get ready to go home. Promptly at four o'clock she let herself out of the house and walked briskly to the station to get her train home to Bromley.

As the train drew slowly out of Victoria, Margaret mused that the day had gone much as usual. The work was at least varied and she had become quite interested herself in the various methods of raising funds for charity, but she had to admit to herself dreading two things. One was "committee" days. Most of the ladies who interested themselves in what Mrs. Hollis describes as "deserving causes" were, like herself, only concerned with the help they could give. However, there were one or two who, in Margaret's opinion, only did so for the publicity they could get out of it. Two such were a Mrs. Miln-Prescott and her daughter Blanche, in some way distantly related to Mrs. Hollis. The other thing

Margaret dreaded were the times when Mrs. Macgennis and Cook had one of their periodic feuds. It usually fell to Margaret to keep the peace until the two ladies felt honour had been satisfied and they were on speaking terms again.

Margaret shrugged off her unwelcome thoughts as she alighted at her station. She walked home quickly through the mild autumn evening. Now in late September, the nights were beginning to draw in and the leaves to fall.

As she put her key in the lock, Mrs. Grant called a "Hello, dear!" from the kitchen. Margaret walked down the hall and into the cosy room. As she kissed her mother's cheek she admonished mildly, "Now why don't you leave everything until I get back?"

"I was only laying the table, dear. Even a semi-cripple can do that."

Margaret patted her mother as she passed her to go and put her coat and hat away.

She returned after a few minutes, put on an apron, and began to prepare the evening meal, which her mother liked to have early.

"Anything interesting happen today?" Mrs. Grant inquired.

"Not really," said Margaret, as she arranged a mixed grill in the pan. "Mrs. Hollis did ask how you were getting on though, and I told her I thought the physiotherapy was doing you good."

"Oh, it is! Mrs. Willis thinks my fingers are getting much more flexible."

Mrs. Willis came in each day to get Mrs. Grant's lunch, and tidy the flat. She had been their daily help years ago when Margaret's father had been alive. She had left to get married, but when her family were old enough to go to school, she had come back to "do" for them, as she called it. She was a veritable treasure, and Margaret often wondered what they would have done without "Willie".

Next morning, when she arrived with the coffee, Margaret saw that Mrs. Macgennis was what Jean, Margaret's young sister, always described as "pregnant with news". Hardly had she placed the tray on the desk then her obvious excitement became too much for her.

"Miss Grant, dear, you'll never guess! Mr. Nicholas is coming home, and for nine months at least this time, so he says. His mother, bless her, is delighted. As are we all, to be sure. Now phwat do you think of that for me piece of morning' news?" She continued, a reminiscent light in her eye. "There'll be a girl or two in this town will go out and buy themselves a new dress when they hear, I'll be bound."

"Will they?" asked Margaret, her brows rising in surprise.

"Indade and they will." The brogue was becoming more pronounced as Mrs. Macgennis continued excitedly. "Didn't I always say Mr. Nicholas received all the sauce and blarney for himself and poor dear Dr. Miles as well? Charm the birds off the bushes would my Mr. Nicky."

Margaret didn't answer. She'd heard a lot about "Mr. Nicholas" in the past from Mrs. Macgennis. How he'd fallen out of a tree while on holiday in Ireland and cut his head open; how his shoelaces had always been undone. Endless boyhood tales had been told, but never this one. Margaret knew that he had been married at the early age of twenty-one and widowed in nine months. Or was it widowered? Mrs. Macgennis had told the story with tears in her eyes of how the young Mrs. Hollis had been killed driving into the country one evening.

Since Mrs. Macgennis was obviously waiting for some remark, Margaret said, "When is he coming home? Soon?"

"Oh, yes! In a week or so. And I wonder now what he'll think of you." But I mustn't stop talking here. There's his room must be got ready."

11

She bustled out, and Margaret smiled to herself. She knew quite well that the preparing of the room would consist of Mrs. Macgennis harrowing the long-suffering daily help nearly to death, and then when everything was absolutely spotless, deciding it wouldn't do and having everything done over again. She wondered idly what she had meant by her remark "I wonder what he'll thing of you." There was no reason for "Mr. Nicholas" to think anything. She was his mother's secretary and general factotum and he would probably not give her more than a passing glance.

Mrs. Hollis was more vague than usual that morning. She did not mention her son's visit until lunchtime, when she suddenly asked Margaret to postpone a committee meeting for the following Tuesday "as I shall be at the airport meeting my son. I expect Nannie told you he was coming home."

As Margaret looked up, she recognized the quizzical expression in her employer's eyes and her own face crumpled into laughter.

"Yes, she did mention it, as a matter of fact."

"I thought so. Nicholas was always her favourite, though she pretends he isn't."

Margaret went down to her office to phone the cancellations. As she dialled the number of Mrs. Miln-Prescott, she wondered if Blanche would be one of those Nannie predicted would be buying a new dress when she heard of Nicholas Hollis's arrival.

When Margaret reached home that evening, she found her sister, Jean sitting with their mother. Playing on the floor were her three-year-old twins. As soon as they saw their aunt, the boys flung themselves at her, and in five minutes Margaret, her hair wildly dishevelled, was playing on the floor with them. Mrs. Grant glanced from one girl to the other. Hard to believe, she thought, that Jean was three years younger. It was Margaret who looked the babe. Indeed, Margaret, her red-brown hair all over the place, looked at

12

that moment no more than a schoolgirl. Eventually she struggled to her feet, a boy under each arm.

"Going to stop for a meal, Jean?" she asked.

"No, I only stayed long enough to say hallo to you. I must get these brats home. Clive will be in around six tonight."

By the time goodbyes had been said, the visitors had gone and the evening meal prepared and eaten, Margaret had quite forgotten Mrs. Macgennis's news of the morning. Usually she related all the things which happened during her day's work knowing full well how restricted was her mother's life. As she was clearing the table she suddenly remembered.

"Goodness, Mother, I almost forgot to tell you. Mrs. Macgennis was full of excitement today. Mrs. Hollis's elder son is coming home next week."

"Oh? I wonder what he is like."

"No idea," Margaret answered as she lifted the tray. "Like the doctor, I expect." Then as she went out of the room she turned her head over her shoulder and, her eyes alight with amusement, said:

"Maybe he's bald too. They do say alopecia runs in families."

"Horrible girl!" Mrs. Grant launghed as her daughter went out with the tray.

But it was some time before Margaret's curiosity was satisfied. Mrs. Hollis displayed no undue excitement at her son's proposed visit, and both she and Margaret were kept fully occupied for the next few days on a project to raise funds for a special Red Cross appeal. As she left the house on the following Tuesday, Margaret saw several suitcases in the hall, but it was not until the Friday of that week that she actually met Nicholas Hollis face to face.

It had been a particularly busy day. As well as all the usual daily chores and mail, it had been the day when Margaret paid the monthly household accounts. Though most of them could be paid by cheque, some of the tradesmen liked to be paid in cash, and in addition, as it was Friday, she had the wage packets to make up.

He usual custom was to borrow a large tray from the kitchen, on which she methodically set out the invoices, cheques, cash and any other items of correspondence which might require discussion with Mrs. Hollis. Having arranged everything to her satisfaction, Margaret opened her office door and crossed the hall. As she reached the staircase, the front door opened briskly and a gale of cold autumn air caught Margaret's pile of carefully arranged accounts. She put out a quick arm and stopped them flying off the tray, but as she did so, her elbow caught the newel post, the tray tilted, and the whole lot slid in one glorious confusion to the floor, silver and notes cascading all over the lower stairs and hall.

Margaret gave a sharp exclamation of distress and started to gather everything up as quickly as she could. She was reaching for a shilling which had lodged itself on its edge on the bottom step, when she becme aware of a pair of trousered legs about a foot away. She subsided on to the step and looked slowly upwards. The man standing before her was of medium height. He had closely cropped black hair, a very brown face and deep-set eyes. Those grey eyes were familiar to Margaret. At the moment they held a decided twinkle and also she thought she detected a look of surprise. She knew instinctively who this man must be. She was about to introduce herself when he spoke.

"Now I know who you must be! My mother often writes to me about her Girl Friday. You must be the incomparable Miss Grant who never makes a mistake or ever does anything wrong."

He was laughing openly now. "May I bring this half-crown to your notice?" and he held out the coin to her.

Margaret was furious, more with herself than with him, but to her chagrin knew that her anger must be showing on her face. True, she had not particularly wanted to go out of her way to try and impress the unknown son, but all the same she could not have made his acquaintance in more undignified circumstances. That he should have laughed and made a remark about her proven efficiency when she was on her knees clearing up piles of scattered money and correspondence made her hot with shame.

When she spoke her voice was stiff. "How do you do. You'll forgive me if I go and clear up this mess?"

Without waiting for a reply, she picked up the tray and vanished into her office.

It was some fifteen minutes later when Margaret entered her employer's sitting-room and laid the re-arranged tray on the desk. As she turned away the door opened and her antagonist strolled into the room.

Mrs. Hollis looked up. "Margaret, I don't think you've met my elder son, have you? Nicholas, this is Miss Grant," and she smiled her delightful smile, the grey eyes, so like this man's that Margaret had immediately recognized him, lighting up.

Margaret mumbled a few words, relieved to find that he didn't appear to be going to reveal the fact that they had already met, and in what circumstances. She hardly heard his answering "How do you do," as she hurried to reach the handle, but he turned quickly and opened the door for her. Margaret passed him, aware that he was still looking at her and that his face now wore a rather mocking smile.

Later that afternoon, as she hurried to the station, the thought crossed her mind that if Nicholas Hollis had, in fact, inherited all the family charm, it was not apparent to her. I wonder though why he looked surprised when he saw me? she thought. Maybe he was expecting me to be older. Then suddenly realizing that she had only five minutes in which to catch her train, she dismissed Nicholas Hollis from her mind and ran the last few yards to the station.

However, during the evening, her mother's inquiries

as to how the day had gone brought it to her mind again.

"I met the elder son today, Mother."

"Did you like him?"

"Well, I only saw him for a couple of minutes. Mrs. Hollis introduced him just as I was leaving."

Somehow she didn't want to tell Mrs. Grant of her prior meeting with Nicholas Hollis, and in order to avoid further questions on the subject she suddenly asked if Jean had phoned.

"Yes. She wants us to go for lunch on Sunday. I said we would. You'd like that, darling, wouldn't you? Clive says he'll pick us up after church."

Sunday was a lovely day, warm for the time of the year. Margaret and her mother walked to church through the park. The flower beds were a mass of Michaelmas daisies and dahlias, a sight to lift the spirits with their variety of bright, glowing colours. When they reached home after the service, they found Jean's husband, Clive, waiting for them. As soon as the car drew up outside her daughter's house, Mrs. Grant's grandsons erupted through the front door. Granny was always certain to have some special surprise in her pockets for her only grandchildren, and today was no exception. While one boy unearthed a packet of chocolate drops from one pocket, the second twin dipped his hand into the other pocket and produced two small model cars. Jean laughed as she assisted her mother over the step.

"You shouldn't let them, you know, Mother."

Mrs. Grant nodded towards her grandsons. "Better take those sweets away, Jean dear, before their lunch. I'm sorry—I should have hidden them in my handbag until later."

Margaret took the coats and hats upstairs, and then came down to give a hand with the preparation for lunch. She was just peeping into the saucepans on the stove when Jean came into the kitchen. The sisters were not very alike. Jean, the younger by three years, was a

16

pretty brunette. As she looked at her sister, Margaret thought it no wonder that Clive had snapped her up and married her at eighteen. He was the son of Mr. Grant's old friend and former partner and as soon as he had qualified as a solicitor he had asked Jean to marry him. She had known him all her life and they had easily persuaded Mrs. Grant to give her consent.

The marriage had been a great success, and the arrival of twin boys two years later had set the seal on their happiness.

I wish it were me, Margaret thought as she looked at her sister's flushed cheeks and bright eyes. I'm getting to be a real old maid.

She turned quickly to test the potatoes, determined to shake off her unusual attack of selfpity. After all, she thought to herself, I could have married Basil Norris five years ago if I'd wanted. Instead I said no before he left for Kuala Lumpur. Anyway, she consoled herself, someone had to take care of Mother.

She shook off her depression and determined to enjoy the day. Later, playing horses on the lawn with Paul and Keith, no one would have taken her for more than sixteen, never mind an old maid. Her hair was hanging in her eyes and the boys had kissed off all her make-up. As she stood a minute later, a boy struggling under either arm, Margaret little guessed how both her mother and sister were each thinking what a pity it was she hadn't married and had children of her own.

CHAPTER TWO

NEXT morning, however, as she walked briskly from the station, all depressing thoughts were banished from her mind. Margaret was already pigeon-holing all the jobs ahead of her in what promised to be an unusually busy day. She let herself in and started at once on the morning's mail.

She had just slit the last envelope when Mrs. Macgennis arrived with the coffee. She was hardly inside the room before saying, "And what did Himself say to you?"

Margaret looked up, for a moment completely bewildered by the question. Then she realized that somehow Mrs. Macgennis was aware of the meeting between Nicholas Hollis and herself, and for some reason wanted to know, not Margaret's own, but Nicholas's reactions to that meeting.

A puzzled frown appeared in her eyes but she only replied:

"He seemed a little surprised, I thought, to see me. Though he knew of me from Mrs. Hollis. He told me so."

Mrs. Macgennis folded her arms, hands under each elbow. She ignored the second half of Margaret's reply.

"Seemed surprised, did he? Well, now!" and to Margaret's surprise, instead of stopping for her customary lengthy chat she walked out of the room chuckling softly to herself.

Margaret gazed at the closed door for a moment, but then looking down at the pile of letters awaiting her attention, she shrugged off her curiosity at Mrs. Macgennis's strange manner, and went back to work.

She was gathering up the letters and folders preparatory to leaving her employer's sitting-room after the morning's dictation, when Mrs. Hollis suddenly said, "By the way, Margaret, didn't you work for an engineering firm before you came here?"

"Why, yes, I did." Margaret knew her voice held surprise.

Mrs. Hollis moved some papers around on her desk

18

and looked more vague than usual. Margaret couldn't help feeling it covered slight embarrassment.

"I wonder then if you'd do some secretarial work for my son? He's been asked as he's in the U.K. just now, to prepare a report for one of the Ministries."

Margaret looked down at her hands for a moment, hardly knowing how to reply. She did not want to refuse her employer's request, but on the other hand, thought the incident had been partially her own fault, she couldn't feel that she had come out of last Friday's episode very creditably, and as a result she did not relish any closer contact with the man who had witnessed her fall from grace. While she was still hesitating, Mrs. Hollis spoke again.

"I'll tell Nicholas to come and talk it over with you then, shall I?"

The phone rang before Margaret could answer, and as Mrs. Hollis picked up the receiver, she collected her papers and went downstairs very thoughtfully.

While she was having her lunch, she turned the problem over in her mind. Since Mrs. Hollis herself had asked her and was therefore willing to give up some of Margaret's time to her son's needs, it was going to be practically impossible to refuse. Margaret again felt the unaccustomed depression and restlessness stealing over her as it had on the previous day. Determined to throw it off, she repaired her make-up, tidied her hair and, putting on her coat, went out for half an hour's fresh air before she started the afternoon's work.

Later that afternoon, as she was transcribing the last letter in her shorthand notebook, the door opened. Although the door was behind her, in the tall mirror over the fireplace she was able to see who had entered the room. She typed deliberately to the end of the line before she turned.

Nicholas Hollis was standing just inside the room watching her. He did not speak for a moment, but stood regarding her in deliberate appraisal. Then as

Margaret said inquiringly, "Yes?" He replied bluntly, "My mother tells me that you are prepared to do some typing for me."

"Mrs. Hollis mentioned that you would like me to do some work for you, yes. But we haven't had time to discuss it properly."

"Well, I'm here instead to discuss it now. You are familiar with engineering terms, I understand. Will you type a report for me?"

"I did three years with an engineering firm before I came here," Margaret answered, "but I don't know if I would be able to manage what you would require."

He smiled suddenly. "Well, I'm sure you could." His eyes suddenly gleamed with malicious fun. "Friday's events were, I feel sure, the exception and not the rule."

He burst out laughing as he saw Margaret's look of horrified surprise. She was quite taken aback. What an objectional man, she thought; he might have spared me that remark.

She felt miserably ill at ease and she knew her face had flushed, but she looked straight at him and said, "The matter was only mentioned to me at lunchtime. You do know, don't you, that for personal reasons I can't stay after four o'clock?"

Nicholas Hollis nodded. He had stopped laughing and he stood for a few moments and looked unsmilingly at her. In fact he stared so hard that Margaret began to fidget with the pile of completed letters beside her. Suddenly he said, "It's not a difficult piece of work. I'd be most grateful if you'd help me out."

The words surprised Margaret and she looked up quickly. She couldn't help a quizzical smile dawning in her eyes as she replied, "Very well, Mr. Hollis. Perhaps you would arrange with Mrs. Hollis when she can spare me to do it."

He nodded and went out, slamming the door to behind him.

Margaret sat down again at her typewriter, but she was a minute or two before she started work again. What a strange man he was! She couldn't quite make him out. Mrs. Macgennis had remarked frequently on his charm. I don't notice it, Margaret said to herself. Perhaps I'm lacking in appreciation or something. Though he does laugh with his eyes, she finally admitted to herself.

That night, as she was getting ready for bed, Margaret studied her face in the bathroom mirror. She approved the straight little nose, the well-shaped mouth. But I'm ordinary, Margaret thought to herself. The brown eyes regarded their reflection sadly. Perhaps our chemistry doesn't mix, an inner voice said, and then Margaret mentally shook herself for allowing her thoughts to return to a man who, so far, in the short time she had known him, had already made her lose both her temper and her dignity. She turned away from the mirror and going into her bedroom, picked up a book and got into bed. Better to read herself into a happier frame of mind before settling down for the night.

Next day, when she took the letters up to Mrs. Hollis, Margaret could not help wondering if Nicholas had told his mother about their conversation in the office downstairs. Nothing in her employer's manner, however, gave anything away. She seemed more than usually gay this morning, and Margaret could not help wishing she had known her when she was a girl. She had often studied the beautiful painting of Mrs. Hollis, done at the time of her marriage, which hung in the long drawing room. Her hair then had been as black as her elder son's.

As if she had read Margaret's thoughts, Mrs. Hollis suddenly said, "I hear it's all fixed up about your helping Nicholas. I'll try and keep my letters short this week. After that Red Cross meeting on Friday, we should be a bit quieter, shouldn't we?"

"Yes, things ought to quieten down once Friday is over. When does Mr. Hollis wish me to do his work? During the afternoons would be easier for me, but of course it's up to him."

"You ask him, Margaret," Mrs. Hollis answered as she turned some letters over on the desk. "Arrange it between the two of you. I'm going to try and take things a little easier while Nicholas is home. I intend telling the committee so on Friday."

Margaret sighed to herself as she went downstairs. The next few months were not going to pass with the smoothness of the last three years, she felt sure. Although he'd been in the house less than a week, already Nicholas Hollis was making his presence felt.

She was just closing her office door as she left for home that afternoon, when the front door bell rang. She opened it to admit Mrs. Miln-Prescott and her daughter to the house. Blanche Miln-Prescott never believed in wasting courtesy on those she regarded as servants. She was a tall blonde, always expensively dressed, and today she was wearing a tweed suit with a small fur collar which made Margaret green with envy.

As the two women entered the hallway, the library door opened and Nicholas Hollis came out, reading a letter as he did so.

Margaret stood in amazement as Blanche pushed past her, and with a "Nicholas darling! Why haven't you phoned?" ran across the wide hall and threw her arms round him. Margaret was treated to her first sample of the famous charm. As if in a dream, she watched him smile beguilingly and, putting his arm round Blanche, kiss her cheek. Then, putting her gently aside, he went across and did the same to Mrs. Miln-Precott.

Margaret waited until all three had started up the stairs before she moved. As she did so she noticed the door to the kitchen closing stealthily. Had Mrs. Macgennis been quietly watching? Had she too seen the fatuous expressions on the faces of the two ladies?

22

Margaret thought as she closed the front door quietly behind her and ran down the steps. She felt a giggle rising. You're getting to be quite a cat, she told herself. Still, it was good to know that the icy Miss Miln-Prescott had a melting point after all.

That night, as they were having supper, Margaret entertained her mother with an account of the incident. Mrs. Grant knew already that Blanche Miln-Prescott never missed an opportunity to snub anyone she considered a social inferior, and many times she had told Margaret she was foolish to permit her to do so.

"Oh, I don't care, Mother," Margaret had answered on one occasion. "She's just an idiotic snob, and in any case she never does it when Mrs. Hollis is there."

On Thursday morning, as Margaret was inserting her key in the lock, the door opened. Thinking Mrs. Macgennis had heard her footsteps, she looked up, ready to smile a "good morning". The smile died out of her eyes when they alighted on the man standing holding the door open. To her disgust she could feel the hot colour rushing into her face. All the sparkle died out of her eyes and murmuring a quick, shy "good morning", she walked past him, hoping that he would not notice the blush. She was walking rapidly in the direction of her office when his voice arrested her.

"Would two o'clock be too early to make a start on my report, Miss Grant?"

Margaret turned slowly. She opened her mouth to say she didn't know how busy the morning would be, and then quickly the thought crossed her mind that it would be more discreet to offer no argument. "No. Two o'clock will be all right. I'll be ready," and she turned and walked into her office.

As she took off her coat she realized that there had been no repetition of the charming smile he had bestowed on the Miln-Precotts. He hadn't even acknowledged her reply. Almost before she had her office door open she heard the front door slam. Mannerless and lacks sympthy, she thought as she took up the letter opener. Then with a rueful smile she thought, but apparenty only to me.

Two o'clock came, but with no sign of Nicholas Hollis. Half an hour later, Margaret's office door was flung open and he strode in, his black brows almost meeting in a frown.

"I hate unpunctual women. I thought you said you'd be ready by two o'clock. It's now half past."

"I've been ready since two," Margaret replied.

"Then perhaps you'd honour me with your company in the library, Miss Grant." He stopped speaking for a moment and looked down at her. Margaret saw him start to smile. It was like the "smile on the face of the tiger". "Unless," he continued in a soft drawl, "you expect me to shout to you from across the hall?"

Margaret was by this time as angry as he. Not bothering to reply she picked up her notebook and pencils and preceded him across the hall and into the library without a word. She walked over to the fire and sat down. Opening her notebook, she looked up, her face stony.

Nicholas Hollis closed the library door and walked over to the table. He picked up a sheaf of papers and started to dictate. While he did so, he prowled to and fro, never once looking at the girl seated by the fire. He had a deep, pleasant, almost hypnotic voice, and once her anger had died down, Margaret found it pleasant to be working with a man once again.

For over an hour he walked back and forth, while her pencil travelled steadily over page after page of her notebook.

As suddenly as he had commenced dictating he stopped. "Can you do a rough draft of that and let me have it by tomorrow?"

Margaret looked at her watch. There was just time to finish off her usual work and catch the train. Tomorrow afternoon the Red Cross meeting was scheduled. She knew that if she was to get this mass of notes typed by tomorrow morning, she would have to do them tonight. She supressed a sigh, however, as she answered, "Yes, it will be ready by one tomorrow." When she reached the door she turned for a moment. "I'll give it to Mrs. Macgennis to take to you as soon as it's ready and then there can be no question of it going astray."

Nicholas didn't reply, but by the faintest glimmer of a smile in his eyes, Margaret knew that he realized this was her retaliation for his accusation that she had kept him waiting. Did he appreciate her refraining from pointing out that she had not been told he wished to dictate to her in the library at two? Somehow she doubted it.

Margaret went back to her office and finished her afternoon's work. Before leaving for home, she looked out the portable typewriter she sometimes took to meetings. Putting her notebook, paper and carbons in a large envelope, she set out for Bromley.

When Mrs Grant saw her come in burdened with this unusual load, her eyes widened. "Goodness, darling. Whatever have you got there?"

"Im afraid it's a typewriter, Mother. You won't mind if I do some typing after supper, will you? I could take it into the bedroom if it will disturb you."

"Don't be silly—of course I shan't mind. This is unusual, though. Is Mrs. Hollis so busy?"

"No. This is for the son."

"Dr. Miles, or the other one?"

"The other one," Margaret replied shortly as she started for the kitchen. Mrs. Grant raised her eyebrows as she followed her daughter out of the sitting-room. It was not like sunny-tempered Margaret to be so brusque. She wondered what had happened to make her so, but tactfully asked no further questions.

While Mrs. Grant laid the table, Margaret made feather-light omelettes and a salad. She opened a tin of fruit and cut bread. With the coffee on a low light, she carried the tray into the dining-room.

They talked as they ate, but Mrs. Grant noticed Margaret did not mention her job, nor tonight did she relate any amusing anecdotes. Something must have happened to annoy her daughter considerably.

When the supper dishes were washed and put away, Margaret opened the typewriter and started work. For two hours she typed on, only raising her head when her mother rose from the chair beside the fire.

"Goodness, Mother! Going to bed already?"

"It's nearly ten o'clock, my dear. You've been so busy you haven't noticed the time. Yes, I think I will go to bed. I'm feeling rather tired."

Margaret got up and followed her mother out of the room. While Mrs. Grant prepared for bed, Margaret filled hot water bottles and heated milk. When she had seen Mrs. Grant comfortably tucked into bed, she went back into the sitting-room and sat down at the typewriter again.

The next time she looked at the clock, it was nearly midnight. The draft was finished and had been read through. When Margaret had corrected the odd typing mistakes she found, she stood up and rubbed her back. She was yawning as she closed the typewriter and went into the kitchen to lay her mother's breakfast tray and put everything ready for the morning.

The next day was hectically busy. Margaret handed the folder containing the draft report to Mrs. Macgennis before she left with Mrs. Hollis to attend the committee meeting. It was mid afternoon before this was over, and she went straight home.

She saw no sign of Nicholas Hollis until the following Wednesday. She was drinking morning coffee and talking to Mrs. Macgennis when he walked into the office. He stopped abruptly just inside the door when he saw she was not alone, and then a small mischievous smile curled his lips. "Never talking, Mac?"

"Go on with you, Master Nicky! Don't you know a wee gossip is the breath of life to me? And who better to have it with than a bonny colleen like our Miss Grant?"

Nicholas did not answer. His smile deepened, but he did not turn his head to look at Margaret. Instead he took hold of Mrs. Macgennis and propelled her towards the door.

"Out, Mac! Out!" he said, as he opened the door. "There's work to be done by your bonny colleen."

He closed the door behind her and came back to Margaret's desk. She sat looking up at him a little apprehensively. Nicholas was frowning again as he opened the folder in his hand. "I've altered this draft considerably and I'd like to add to it, if you could spare the time," he said as he drew up a chair and sat down on the other side of the desk.

"I usually go up to your mother at this time," Margaret replied. "Could it possibly wait until after lunch?"

"I'm afraid not. I'll fix it with Mother." And before she could protest further, Nicholas had lifted the house telephone and was talking to Mrs. Hollis.

"Quite all right. You can do her letters later," he said as he put the telephone down, and without waiting for any comment from Margaret, he began explaining to her where he wanted the report altered.

Margaret could feel the indignation rising, but she resolutely fought it down. Any attempt she had so far made to come to grips with this man had ended with confusion and embarrassment to herself.

While she had been talking earlier, Mrs. Macgennis had switched on the second bar of the electric fire. The room was beginning to feel unpleasantly warm and Margaret found herself more and more frequently stifling yawns as the dictation continued. Nicholas Hollis's voice was deep and soothing. Combined with the heat it was producing almost a soporific effect.

Stifling yet another yawn, Margaret looked up to find Nicholas watching her closely.

"Are you tired, Miss Grant?"

Margaret smiled. "No, not really . . ." She was just about to explain how warm she felt and apologize for yawning when Nicholas looked away from her and said gently, almost negligently, "Then please don't yawn while I'm dictating."

Before Margaret could utter the angry retort which was almost choking her, he started to dictate once more. Automatically, she recommenced to take down his words, her back rigid with anger and two bright spots of colour in her cheeks. Her face was still flushed several minutes later when he finally stopped speaking and put the draft down on the desk. As he rose to go she could feel tears at the injustice of his remark beginning to well up in her eyes, and she turned quickly away so that he would not see she was on the verge of weeping. I hate him! she thought as she gazed through the window, seeing the small garden through a blur of tears.

The door opened and closed behind her. Margaret took out a handkerchief and blew her nose. As she wiped her eyes it occurred to her that she loathed Nicholas Hollis as much for the fact that he could reduce her so easily to tears as to what he had actually said.

As she tucked the handkerchief away again a voice spoke softly directly behind her.

"I'm sorry I've made you cry. I didn't think you'd take my words so much to heart. You're not going to tear up my draft now and throw it in the waste paper basket to show what you think of me, now are you?"

Margaret stood absolutely still for the space of half a minute before she turned round. Nicholas Hollis was standing, hands in pockets, smiling whimsically.

Is he turning on the charm because he's afraid I won't do his precious report? was the thought that crossed Margaret's mind.

She walked past him and sat down at her typewriter. As she opened her notebook she said quietly, "Don't worry. I wouldn't do anything so childish. And I wasn't

28

crying because of what you said, but because I have a headache."

"Oh, I see. Well, I apologize again, not only for being mistaken about the cause of the tears, but also for misjudging you. Am I forgiven?"

Margaret said quickly, "Yes, of course," and putting paper in her machine, started to type. She knew Nicholas stood watching her for several minutes before he walked out of the room, but she did not raise her head even when the door opened and closed for the second time.

That night, Margaret had difficulty in getting to sleep. She lay, her hands under her head, staring into the darkness. In her mind she went over the scene again and again. Detestable man, she thought, I'm sure he only apologized when he saw I was thoroughly upset for the sole purpose of making sure his report got finished. I'm sure he wasn't really sorry. It half occurred to her that she was whipping up her anger against him deliberately. As the small unwelcome thought crept in, she turned on her side, trying to dismiss the whole disastrous morning from her mind. Despite her good intentions, sleep proved elusive. Every time she tried to fall asleep, a picture kept coming between her and the darkness. A picture of a thin, brown, intelligent face, the well-shaped mouth just touched with a smile as he had asked her pardon. I wish he'd stayed in Rhodesia, was her thought as she turned her pillow over and pounded it into a more comfortable position.

The normality of the morning's routine calmed her. By the time she had dressed her mother, made breakfast, cleared away and got herself ready to catch her train, a calmness had descended on her. She found she had the afternoon free to finish the report, and as she read through the final copy, she had to admit that it was good. Clear and concise, written in a blunt astringent style, it was vastly different from some of the dull and often obtuse reports she had often been called upon

29

to prepare. She had begun the work for Nicholas Hollis with a good deal of reluctance. She had to admit to herself though that despite her antipathy for its author the work had caught her interest. From his mother, from the gossip Mrs. Macgennis let fall as she brought in the daily coffee tray, and even from occasional remarks Nicholas himself had made from time to time, Margaret had to admit he was a man of many parts. Following his course in engineering after he had left school, he had done his national service in the Royal Air Force. When this had ended, and presumably also because of his wife's death, he had gone out to Africa to live.

At the start, he had worked on the copper belt, in what had then been Northern Rhodesia, but after two or three years he had gone south to Salisbury where he was now employed by another engineering firm. About this time too, though knowing nothing about farming, he had bought a property about forty miles outside the city. He had installed a farm manager, and in his spare time had picked up a good all-round knowledge of agriculture as it was carried out in that part of the world. In twelve months, Nicholas could have run the farm himself, but as he still had a full-time job as well as having been appointed as an adviser to the local government on the development of industrial research in Central Africa, he had kept his farm manager on. His specialized engineering experience, Margaret could see from the report she had typed, must have been invaluable on its own account.

As she put the papers into a clean folder and went to look for Mrs. Macgennis half of her mind reluctantly admitted that perhaps she was just a little bit sorry that the work was finished. Stormy though their meetings invariably were, at least they were never dull. From now on it was unlikely they would come very much in each other's way.

CHAPTER THREE

FRIDAY was Mrs. Grant's birthday. When Margaret carried in her breakfast tray, as well as the dainty china there was a fragrant scarlet rose in a vase beside the teapot.

"Happy birthday, darling!"

Mrs. Grant was already sitting up in bed. "You spoil me, Margaret dear. Oh, what a lovely rose!" and she lifted it to her nose and sniffed appreciatively.

"Here's my present. Jean will be along about ten with hers. You know, don't you, that she's coming to take you back with her for the day, and that we're going to the theatre tonight?"

"Yes. Jean phoned me yesterday and I've told Mrs. Willis to take the day off. It will be lovely. You're coming to the theatre too, aren't you?"

"Now would I miss it?" Margaret laughed. "I shall go straight from town to Jean's, and then Clive will drive us all up to the theatre. Incidentally, I've got another birthday surprise for you. We're going to Bournemouth tomorrow, just the two of us, and staying until Sunday. You'll like that, won't you?"

Tears stood in Mrs. Grant's eyes. "Oh, I shall, my dear. How very sweet of you to think of it. Can I phone Mary today and let her know?"

Mary Salmon was an old school friend of Mrs. Grant's. She was a widow, had no children, and having been crippled with arthritis for many years now lived permanently in a nursing home in Bournemouth. As she was unable to travel, it was only when Jean or

31

Margaret could take their mother down to Hampshire that the two old friends could meet.

Margaret smiled. "No need. I've already written to Aunt Mary and told her we'll be dropping in at tea-time tomorrow. I had a reply yesterday morning. She's delighted she'll be seeing you."

The day went well, and at four o'clock Margaret set off for her sister's house, carrying a change of dress in a small case.

After helping with the twins' tea-time, she went upstairs to change into the fine wool dress she had brought with her. It was in a sage green shade, and with it Margaret wore delicate gold ear-rings and necklace in a leaf pattern, a twenty-first present from Mrs. Salmon, who was her godmother. Jean came into the bedroom as Margaret was combing her hair and nodded approval. "Lovely, Margaret darling. Now what do you think of mine?"

She twirled round so that Margaret could see the royal blue frock she was wearing from all angles. It suited her dark colouring perfectly, and made her blue eyes look darker in comparison.

"No one would dream you were the mother of those boisterous imps downstairs, Jean. You look about eighteen," Margaret said.

"Thank you for those kind words, sister dear. Now, let's hurry. The baby-sitter is here and we don't want to miss the beginning."

They had just got to their seats when the lights dimmed. Margaret had no time to look around before the scene on stage claimed her complete attention. Jean had chosen a new drawing-room comedy, well dressed, well staged and very witty. The audience were enthralled from the start, as the absence of coughing and rustling in chocolate boxes testified. When the lights went up at the close of the first act, Margaret blinked. She had been so immersed in the plot that it was a moment or two before she realized that her sister was speaking to her.

Jean leaned over and said, "Margaret! Isn't that Mrs. Hollis sitting two rows in front?"

Margaret looked in the direction of her sister's glance. She immediately recognized not only Mrs. Hollis, but her two sons, Blanche Miln-Prescott and her mother, and also a niece of Mrs. Hollis in the party. They were all getting up apparently to stretch their legs between now and the beginning of Act Two. Margaret, in the aisle seat, realized they would pass close beside her.

As the party in front rose, Dr. Miles took his mother and Mrs. Miln-Prescott by the arms, and walked them up the aisle. Mrs. Hollis stopped for a moment. "Hello, Margaret! Enjoying the play?"

"Yes, thank you. Very much indeed."

Mrs. Hollis smiled and said "hello" to the rest of Margaret's family before she walked on. Behind her, Nicholas was holding an arm each of his cousin and Blanche Miln-Prescott. As his mother moved on, he nodded briefly to Margaret.

"Who is that?" Jean asked.

Margaret waited until she thought the Hollises and their guests were out of earshot before replying. Hoping Jean would not notice the flush in her cheeks she said, "Oh, that's the elder son, home from Rhodesia."

She sat back in her seat. How could she be so stupid? she thought. Nearly twenty-seven years of age and behaving like an adolescent schoolgirl just because a man she had only known for a fortnight was patronizing the same theatre! Pulling herself together, she determined to dismiss any more thoughts of this nature, and turning to her brother-in-law, she asked him some question at random. To her relief, he didn't seem to notice the high colour in her face, and they chatted amicably until the start of the second act.

Later, standing in the foyer with her mother and Jean, waiting for Clive to fetch the car, Margaret again saw Nicholas Hollis. He came in from the street, his overcoat collar turned up, and almost bumped into them as he pushed open the swing doors. "Hello, Miss Grant," he said, "we meet again."

Margaret introduced her mother and Jean.

"Have you seen my mother?" he asked when he had shaken hands. "I've got two taxis outside and I daren't keep them waiting."

At that moment, Margaret saw Mrs. Hollis and her party coming across the foyer. "Here they are."

"Do you mind if I dash, then? Good night!"

He raised a hand towards his forehead in a caricature of a military salute, and before they could say "good night" in return, he had gone across to his mother and was steering her through the swing doors to the taxis.

"Well!" said Jean. "That was a bit abrupt. Is he always in a hurry?"

Clive arrived at that moment urging them to hurry before he got booked for parking, and Margaret was saved the trouble of replying.

The following morning, Mrs. Grant and Margaret caught an early train, and by lunchtime were sitting down to a meal in a quiet hotel in Bournemouth. It was cold outside, but the sun came out as they strolled later that afternoon in the direction of the nursing home where Mrs. Salmon lived.

"It would be lovely to have a couple of weeks here, wouldn't it?" Mrs. Grant said. "The air is like wine."

"Perhaps we'll be able to afford it in the spring, it will be something to look forward to," Margaret answered.

Her thoughts wandered into the might-have-been as she guided her mother through the gardens. If only her mother had not been persuaded to gamble so foolishly with the investments so carefully made by Margaret's father. He had died when she and Jean were still in their teens, and had it not been for the timely intervention of Clive's father, who was now the senior partner of her father's old firm, Margaret knew that they would have been left quite penniless. As it was, he had salvaged just enough to buy Mrs. Grant an annuity. With Margaret's salary, they were just able to manage, but the money didn't often stretch to extras like autumn holidays. They were very lucky that Jean and Clive took a bungalow at Broadstairs every summer and invited Margaret and Mrs. Grant to share their annual seaside family holiday. It didn't do, Margaret thought, to think of all those "ifs", and she determinedly turned her thoughts to ways and means of saving enough to ensure a holiday for her mother next spring.

On Monday, it was raining hard when Margaret arrived at work, and as she had forgotten her umbrella, she had got very wet on her walk from the station. As she opened the office door, she was halted on the threshold by the sight of Nicholas Hollis sitting with his feet on her desk, quite obviously waiting for her.

She took off her dripping headscarf and gloves and said, "Good morning."

"Good morning, Miss Grant. You're very wet. Here——" he heaved himself to his feet as he spoke, "give me your coat and I'll get it dried."

Margaret slipped off her coat. "No, it's all right. It will soon dry in the cloakroom."

At this moment Mrs. Macgennis came in with the coffee tray. Margaret was amused to notice there were two cups on it. Nicholas took the coat out of Margaret's hands and held it until Mrs. Macgennis had safely put the tray down. Then he handed the coat to her with a "Get it dried, Mac. It's soaking."

He sat down again and poured the coffee into the two cups. When Margaret had dried her face and tidied her hair into some sort of order, she turned from the mirror to find him drinking his coffee and watching her. As she turned round he said, "Here, sit down and have this while it's hot."

It seemed easier to do as he said, and she subsided into a chair on the opposite side of the desk.

"This is very well done. Thank you," he had, she

saw, the report in his hand. "I've had to make two more alerations to this page though." He opened the folder about half way through. "Would you mind doing that one page again, please? Oh, and by the way, we must come to some arrangement as regards payment."

"There's no need, Mr. Hollis." Margaret knew her voice sounded stiff, but she didn't want to get involved in a conversation with this man about money. "Your mother pays me very adequately, and after all, I've done the typing in her time."

Nicholas eyed her for a few moments before he replied. "What are you trying to say, Miss Grant? You wouldn't type a single word for me were it not for my mother having asked?"

Margaret could feel that tell-tale colour rising. She looked him bravely in the eyes as she said, "Maybe something like that."

She knew she sounded silly, even a little sulky, but it was too late now. Before she could stop herself she heard herself saying, "Perhaps instead you'd like to give a donation to one of your mother's charities."

She stopped short, ashamed of herself even as the words left her lips. What could have come over her? Nicholas sat on the other side of the desk, a steely gleam in his grey eyes as he looked at her. Then he got up slowly.

"Well, you really do dislike me, don't you? I thought at first you were pretending."

As the door closed behind him, Margaret let out a gasp. Why had she been so rude to him? He had really been rather nice, taking her wet coat, thanking her for a job well done. She had come out of the encounter rather badly, she felt. Should she apologize? No, that might make things worse.

Cross with herself, she started to slit open the morning's letters, then as the paperknife slipped and made a small cut in her finger, she said to herself, Serve you right! That's what comes of getting into paddies.

When she went upstairs a little later, Mrs. Hollis discussed the play for a few moments before she commenced the morning's work. Margaret explained that the previous day had been her mother's birthday and added, "She doesn't get out much these days, and I think she thoroughly enjoyed the evening."

"I hope she did," Mrs. Hollis replied. "All our small party thought it excellent, even Miles," and her eyes twinkled. Margaret smiled back. Dr. Miles's other-worldliness was a source of constant amusement to the entire household.

Later that day Margaret re-typed the alteration in the report and gave it to Mrs. Macgennis. For the next two or three days, she half hoped, half feared Nicholas would stroll into the office, but she saw no sign of him. Well, at any rate, she thought, he hasn't tried to pay me. It would have been dreadful if he had insisted.

The following Friday, as Mrs. Hollis was going through her correspondence, the phone rang. Margaret rose to go, thinking Mrs. Hollis would not wish her to overhear a private conversation, but she was motioned to sit down again. As she replaced the receiver, Mrs. Hollis said, "That was Nicholas. He went up to stay with friends in Scotland on Wednesday night, and this is the first I've heard from him since. At least I know he's arrived safely."

She smiled ruefully. "Men never think we women may worry, do they? Now, where was I?" and she plunged straight into a discussion with Margaret about the date for the annual cocktail party she gave each December.

This event was more in the nature of a duty than a pleasure for all concerned in its preparation. To it Mrs. Hollis invited all the people with whom she was associated in her charitable work. Margaret had helped organize the last two, had, in fact, attended them herself to see that everything went well. On the rare occasions when she had to be out in the evenings, she

37

arranged either for her sister or Mrs. Willis to come and sit with her mother, and she made a mental note to ask one of them to sit in when the date was finally decided.

For the next three weeks, Margaret saw no sign of her employer's elder son, and could only presume he was still in Scotland. The one person she could have questioned, Mrs. Macgennis, remained strangely silent on the subject of her favourite, the only remarks she made being that "The phone is a deal less noisy now Master Nicholas is away," and on another occasion, "At least with Himself away we don't have Miss Miln-Prescott nearly livin' here."

So that's how the land lies, thought Margaret. I wonder if he's in love with our ice-cold Blanche. They'd make a good pair.

She did not admit to herself that she missed the prospect of a possible passage of arms with Nicholas Hollis, or that his absence could have been the reason why the autumn seemed unusually dark and dreary this year.

On the last day of October, when Margaret knocked at her sitting-room door, she found her employer standing gazing through the window, instead of seated as usual in her favourite chair.

After telling her to sit down, Mrs. Hollis still stood looking across the square and then, as if suddenly making up her mind, she walked across the room and made herself comfortable in the big armchair. She folded her hands in her lap and looked across at Margaret.

"Before we begin work, my dear, I want to ask you a favour. I'm having a dinner party tonight, and I wonder whether you'd come and help me out as another woman at the table. You see, Nicholas has suddenly decided to fly home and he'll be here this evening. Then, last night, I had a call from Mrs. Miln-Prescott saying her

38

daughter would be unable to come as she had to go on urgent business to Scotland."

Mrs. Hollis paused for a moment. Margaret could have sworn that a small sardonic smile, very like that often seen on her elder son's face, shone for a brief moment in her eyes. Then she continued, "It leaves me two women short, and I'd be so very grateful if you'd come and fill in. Could you get your sister to take care of your mother for one evening, do you think?"

Margaret pondered for a moment. "I'm sure I could arrange about Mother. We have a very good daily help who would come in and sit with her. I'd love to come if it would help you at all."

"Oh, it would, my dear. Go along home about three o'clock and I'll arrange for a taxi to come and collect you at a quarter to seven."

When she had finished her lunch, Margaret rang and arranged with Mrs. Willis to come in that evening and keep her mother company. When she finished the call, she put on her coat and walked to the nearest shops where she bought herself some very sheer nylons. She had one presentable dinner dress, given to her by her sister. It was in a warm, chocolate-brown chiffon which Jean had originally bought for herself. It hadn't suited her, and she had given it to Margaret. So far she had never had the opportunity of wearing it.

She was bathed, dressed and in process of doing her face that evening when Mrs. Grant walked into her daughter's bedroom.

"Yes, Margaret, that looks very nice. Now, what are you going to wear for jewellery?"

"I thought my gold necklace," Margaret answered as she carefully applied mascara.

"No," Mrs. Grant said, "wear Papa's jade instead, it will be a much better contrast."

Margaret's grandfather had had business contacts in

the Far East, and on one of his trips many years before, he had brought Mrs. Grant home a very beautiful jade set comprising necklace, bracelet and pendant ear-rings.

"I'd love to wear them, Mother, if you don't mind lending them to me. They're so perfect."

As she took the box from her mother and opened it, Margaret did not see the happy smile on Mrs. Grant's lips. Fond as she was of both her daughters, it was the elder girl with her constant care and devotion who held the greater part of her affections. As Margaret snapped the necklace round her throat, she little realized the trend of her mother's thoughts.

I hope she enjoys herself, Mrs. Grant was thinking. She looks lovely tonight and could hold her own with anyone.

Unaware of what was passing in her mother's mind, Margaret gave a last pat to her hair, and picking up coat and handbag, went over and tucked her arm inside her mother's. "Come along. Let's wait for Willie in the warm, shall we?"

Mrs. Willis and the taxi arrived almost simultaneously. Margaret kissed her mother and said, "I shan't be late, but go to bed at your usual time anyway. If you're still awake when I come in, I'll tell you all about it."

It was just after half past seven when the taxi dropped her off at her destination. She let herself into the house and found Mrs. Macgennis awaiting her at the head of the stairs. As she led Margaret into one of the bedrooms she said, "Really there's no need for me to show you where to put your coat. Miss Grant dear, but I was after wanting to see what like your dress was." As Margaret took off her coat, she continued, "Glory to goodness, girl dear, a picture you are, to be shure!"

"No doubt about it—you've kissed the Blarney stone, Mrs. Macgennis," Margaret laughed as she went to the mirror to see that her hair was tidy. She had to admit to herself, however, that she was looking her best. The fine tucking on the bodice of the dress, the tight bracelet sleeves, and the swirl of the wide skirt somehow made her look taller and more dignified. At least I'll pass, she thought, as she walked towards the door, no matter what beautiful creations the others may wear.

Mrs. Macgennis opened the door of the long drawing-room on the other side of the upper hall and spoke her name. Immediately, Mrs. Hollis came forward and took her hand.

"Now, Margaret, come and meet everyone." She took Margaret over to the fire. On a couch, sitting talking together, were Mrs. Miln-Prescott and Mrs. MacNeil, Mrs. Hollis's sister.

"You know my sister and Mrs. Miln-Prescott, don't you, but I think you haven't met my brother-in-law. Charles, this is a young friend of mine, Margaret Grant."

Margaret shook hands with a tall, grey-haired man, who had risen from a chair. She smiled a shy "good evening" to the two ladies, and then realizing that Miles Hollis was pushing forward a chair for her, thankfully sat down. She was listening to the conversation when she got the feeling she was being watched. Margaret turned her head and saw Nicholas staring at her from across the room.

As soon as she met his eyes, he turned his back and busied himself with an array of bottles and glasses on a small side table.

A moment later he came across the room carrying a tray. He offered it to his aunt and uncle and to Mrs. Miln-Prescott, then strolled over to where Margaret was sitting with his brother. He did not smile as he said, "What will you have, Miss Grant? Sherry? An aperitif? Or would you prefer a gin and something?"

Margaret's face was as unsmiling as his when she looked up. "I'd like a sherry, please. Dry." He nodded and said, "Your usual, Miles?"

Miles agreed, and Nicholas went back to the other side of the room to pour the drinks. Goodness, Margaret thought, is he going to wage a one-man war all the evening? If he is, everyone will notice. She felt her mouth beginning to go dry with apprehension. It looked like being a thoroughly uncomfortable dinner party.

However, as he put a glass into her hand a few minutes later, Margaret looked up to see a charming smile cross his face—the same sort of attractive smile she had seen him give to Blanche Miln-Prescott when he had first greeted her on his return home. Margaret was amazed at the way it softened and altered his face. To her surprise, he drew up a chair at her other side and engaged her in conversation.

Margaret did not remember what they talked about before the next guests arrived and he rose to greet them. She was so stunned at Nicholas Hollis's obvious efforts to charm and entertain her that her contributions to the conversation were almost negligible.

She was introduced to the new arrivals. There were two colleagues of Miles Hollis and a married couple, obviously special friends of Mrs. Hollis. One of the doctors, introduced as William Pettigrew, sat down beside Margaret and asked her if she were an old friend of Miles. They were soon deep in a discussion about a small boy who had recently figured as a newspaper headline. He'd been rushed home from Cyprus with an unidentified blood complaint. Margaret discovered that William Pettigrew nursed several pet theories about a possible cure, and she was very interested to hear a professional man's opinion. The publicity had raised a great deal of interest during the past two weeks, and hardly a newspaper came out without giving the latest development in the fight to save the boy's life.

Margaret was so engrossed in what Dr. Pettigrew was saying that she looked up in surprise when dinner was announced. As they rose, William Pettigrew offered her his arm. He did it in such a solemn, old-fashioned way that Margaret nearly let her sense of the ridiculous overcome her and curtsey back. However, he was a friendly man, and she was relieved to find when they reached the dining-room, that she had been placed between him and Mr. MacNeill.

The dinner was delicious. Although Mrs. Hollis as a rule had very simple meals, Cook, who had been with her for nearly twenty years, could produce, when she felt so disposed, a meal worthy of a first-class chef. They began with melon. Instead of being served in the usual manner with sugar and ginger, this had been cut in rounds, the seeds had been removed and the centre space filled with a savoury concoction of shrimps, grated celery and nut mixed with a piquant sauce. This was followed by a clear soup, and then Mrs. Macgennis carried in a large saddle of mutton. As she put this down in front of Nicholas, Margaret noticed that it had been carved and then rearranged so that at first glance the joint looked untouched. Cook's niece, who had come in specially to help, followed with a selection of vegetables, which she arranged at intervals down the table. Margaret found herself facing a divided tureen containing delicate spears of broccoli on one side and tiny buttered carrots on the other. She was amused to find herself thinking how well the two colours of the vegetables blended with the delicate pattern on the dinner service.

As she watched Nicholas transfer the steaming slices of succulent meat on to plates and hand them round, Margaret admired the speed and dexterity with which he did so. He might have been in the daily habit of attending to the wants of a large family, she thought, instead of being a lone widower.

By the time the bowls of icecream and butterscotch sauce had been brought to the table, Margaret felt she couldn't possibly eat another thing. She refused the sweet but accepted instead a very small biscuit and a sliver of cheese, more to have something to toy with than because she wanted it. Wine had been served during the meal, and she hoped that it wouldn't have an awkward effect on her. She wasn't used to more than an occasional glass of sherry.

However, as she followed the other ladies back to the drawing-room she was relieved to find that she didn't feel the slightest bit giddy as she had feared. When coffee was handed round, Margaret found herself sitting beside Mrs. MacNeill, and she made inquiries after her daughter, who had recently been married. Mrs. Mac-Neill was only too happy to go into details of the wedding and the house to which the newlyweds had returned from their honeymoon. It was apparently situated near Virginia Water, and on Margaret idly saying, "Isn't that near to Ascot?" the conversation immediately turned to fashions.

Margaret soon found herself more or less out of the discussion which followed. Even Mrs. Hollis, who did not often go to the races, reminisced about some of the hats she had worn in "her young days", so that by the time the men came back into the room, Margaret felt she was ready for a change of subject.

Dr. Pettigrew, to her surprise, immediately came across the room and seated himself beside her. As he offered his cigarette case to her, Margaret suddenly looked up to see Nicholas gazing across the room at her, an undeniably quizzical expression in his eyes.

She looked away, but not before, to her intense annoyance, she felt a blush colouring her face.

More coffee was handed round and the talk became general. Dr. Pettigrew proved to be an amusing conversationalist, and even Miles Hollis was induced to tell one or two anecdotes of incidents which had occurred when they were medical students together, which had the whole room in fits of laughter. Margaret was smiling with the rest when a voice said quietly in her ear, "See what you missed not taking up nursing. Life in a hospital sounds as if it's one long round of jollity, and if it can make my staid brother behave as he has just described, think what effect it might not have had on you, my dear Miss Grant!"

Margaret turned quickly to find Nicholas leaning over

the back of her chair, his face not six inches from her own. As she was summoning up a response to this amazing remark, his uncle called across the room, "How was the weather in Scotland, Nicholas?" and he straightened up and walked away to answer Mr. MacNeill. Margaret sat, her eyes on Nicholas's back. He must think she was the most boring of girls to say what he had.

Suddenly Margaret found she had lost all interest in the people sitting around her, and wondered how soon she could politely leave to go home. It was nearly ten-thirty now and the last train left at eleven. As far as she knew, no taxi had been ordered to take her home. As she took a surreptitious glance at her wrist watch, she saw Mrs. Hollis smile reassuringly at her, almost as if she had guessed what Margaret was thinking. At that moment, Mrs. MacNeill rose and said it was time they were leaving, and as she passed Margaret's chair, Mrs. Hollis bent and murmured, "One of the boys will be running you home, my dear."

The protest that rose to Margaret's lips remained unuttered as her employer immediately turned away and followed her sister from the room. In the general move to leave which followed, Margaret slipped from the room and went to fetch her coat. When she came out of the bedroom and passed the drawing-room door, she noticed that Miles and his two friends were still deep in conversation.

Mrs. Hollis was in the hall saying goodbye to Mrs. Miln-Prescott when Margaret came down the stairs. She turned and said, "Ah, there you are, my dear. I think the car is at the door now. Thank you for coming along tonight. It was sweet of you."

"No, no, thank you for inviting me. I've enjoyed it very much," Margaret replied.

Calling a last good night, she ran down the steps. A car was at the kerb and the passenger door open ready. Margaret crossed the pavement and slipped into the seat, guessing as she did so who would be in the driver's seat. Nicholas Hollis's amused grin was quite clear in the light from the street lamps.

"I shall need guiding the last half of the journey. Bromley, isn't it?"

In a small voice, Margaret said "yes", then plucking up her courage, she said, "I still have time to catch the last train. There's no need to drag you so far out at this hour. If you'd just take me to Victoria, I shall be most grateful."

For a few minutes there was no reply. Nicholas continued to drive down Buckingham Palace Road as if she had not spoken. Then he shot her a quick side glance and said, "What, go back and face my mother's wrath? I'd be much too frightened to admit I'd not done as I was asked."

Margaret did not reply to this facetious remark. She contented herself with turning her head away to look through the nearside window and saying in a cold little voice, "Just as you wish, Mr. Hollis."

Nothing more was said for the next few miles and then, as Nicholas hesitated at a crossing, Margaret said, "Right here."

Nicholas swung the wheel to the right, and she glanced at his face. He was looking bored and rather tired. Margaret felt more uncomfortable than ever that he had felt obliged to drive her all this way. I must make an effort to hide the fact that he makes me feel so uncomfortable, she thought, and show I'm grateful to him for driving me home. After all, he could have left it to Miles.

She sought in her mind for some remark she could make to break the silence between them. As she did so, Nicholas spoke.

"I think we go left here, don't we?"

"Yes. Then right at the next traffic lights. The road is fairly straightforward after that." She cleared her throat and continued, "I really am most grateful to

46

you for bringing me all this way. I can see you're tired, and I haven't even made interesting conversation to while away the journey."

"No, you haven't" he nodded.

Margaret was so astonished at his quick agreement that she turned fully towards him for the first time. As he pulled up at the red light, Nicholas turned his head and grinned boyishly.

"But then I don't like prattling women."

Not for the first time, Margaret marvelled at the speed with which he could switch from what bordered on boorishness to the utmost charm. It was almost as if another man now faced her from the one who had looked so indifferent not two minutes ago.

"Do you know, my sweet, you behave half the time like a sulky little girl who needs a good spanking."

"And the other half?" she inquired sweetly.

"Hm! I wouldn't like to hazard a guess. You're generally so quiet when I'm around, but you may have hidden depths for all I know."

He sounded as if he had lost interest already as he changed gear and the car moved forward.

They reached Margaret's home without any further verbal sparring, and as she waited for him to come and help her out, Margaret looked for her key. Nicholas helped her out and taking the key out of her hand, he walked up the garden path and opened the front door. As he handed the key back to her, Margaret looked up at him.

"Thank you once again, Mr. Hollis."

He sketched her a brief salute. "Think nothing of it, Miss Grant," and he was gone, down the path and into the car.

CHAPTER FOUR

IT was nearly a week later before they met again. Margaret was finishing a long list of envelopes, a task which always irritated her, when the door opened suddenly and Nicholas strode into the room. He hooked out a chair from under the table with one foot, and sat down.

"Think you could dash out half a dozen letters?" he asked brusquely.

"Anything to put off these envelopes," Margaret replied quickly.

His brows rose. "The lady is human after all! I thought you were wedded to good works."

Margaret's mouth tightened.

"Ah, now you're going into one of your little-girl sulks!"

She suddenly realized that he was doing his best to make her lose her temper again, and she looked up from her notebook. From the gleam in his eyes, it was obvious he was about to be as rude and outrageous as possible. I'll call his bluff, she thought.

A mischievous smile lit her eyes. "I shouldn't administer the spanking even if I am," she said. "Mrs. Macgennis wouldn't approve at all."

There was an instant's complete silence and then Nicholas let out a bark of laughter. He bowed slightly and said, his voice sounding deeper even than usual, "Round one to you, my lady."

Margaret smoothed out the page of her notebook and poised her pencil over it. Nicholas saw the action and turned away, looking down at the papers in his hand. Without delaying further, he began dictating his correspondence.

Later that afternoon, he put his head round the office door to see if she had finished his letters. Margaret was just completing the last one, and as she pulled it out of her typewriter, she sighed softly. Nicholas was standing beside the window, reading through the completed letters, but he looked up. "Sad?"

"No. Just a bit tired. It's been a busy day. Lots of awkward people phoning," Margaret replied.

"And awkward people piling more work on you?"

Margaret laughed as she got up and walked to the window to check through the letters she held in her hand. The brief winter afternoon was drawing to an end, and she had not yet put on the electric lights.

As she stood, almost elbow to elbow with Nicholas Hollis as they both read the letters they held, a peculiar feeling began to steal over her. She could see the hand holding the paper begin to shake, and she closed her eyes momentarily.

It could be, she thought. I, the emotionally steady daughter, devoted to work and home. I can't be shaking like this merely because I'm standing beside a member of the opposite sex. It's ridiculous!

But ridiculous or not, Margaret moved quickly back to her desk, and in case Nicholas should notice, pretended to be altering a word in the letter. As she stared unseeingly at the paper before her, she remembered Nannie Macgennis saying, "Charm the birds off the bushes, would Mr. Nicky." Certainly the magnetism emanating from him a moment before had been almost tangible.

The sooner he goes back to Africa the better, was her thought as she placed the letter down for his signature. She watched him through her lashes as he quietly finished reading through the pile of correspondence she had typed for him.

He looks so insignificant really, she mused. He's not

good-looking and he's only of medium height, not much taller than me. And that hair—it's like a scrubbing brush. I must be going mad!

As if in answer to her thoughts, Nicholas placed the last letter on the pile and turned to look at her. As his eyes met hers, Margaret immediately cancelled out all her previous thoughts. Seeing the expression in those dark, intelligent eyes as he thanked her, no one could have called him insignificant, and when he went out of the room, it suddenly seemed to Margaret that the winter afternoon seemed greyer than before. She shook herself, and with a muttered, "Don't be a complete fool," busied herself with the rest of the usual afternoon tasks.

But later that night, when sleep proved elusive, she found herself thinking once again of the afternoon's incident. Lying, her hands linked behind her head, she stared into the darkness and mentally castigated herself for her foolishness.

I couldn't be so stupid as to fall for a man I don't even like, she thought, and of all men, Nicholas Hollis. If I were the only girl left in London, he wouldn't even look at me.

Mrs. Hollis's cocktail party for the members of the various committees on which she served had now been fixed for the second week in December. Margaret had arranged for her mother to be looked after that evening so that she could stay and help. In addition to the cocktail party, there were the Christmas parties for the crippled and spastic children's homes to be fixed up, and in the sudden influx of work, it was a day or two before Margaret had time to breathe. From arriving at work in the morning until she left to catch her train, it seemed an endless race against the clock to get all the hundred and one items attended to. It didn't help either that the phone seemed to ring non-stop.

hunched into it. The legs were wrapped in a tartan rug

50

recalled she had not seen Nicholas Hollis since the day she had become aware of what Nannie Macgennis would have referred to as "the cratur's fatal charm". Almost as if some telepathy were at work, the next time she was in her employer's sitting-room, Mrs. Macgennis came in holding a large pile of magazines. Her tone was so lugubrious as she said, "The magazines have arrived. Shall I take them in to him?" that Margaret looked up in surprise.

Mrs. Hollis laughed. "As bad as that, is he, Nannie?"

Mrs. Macgennis's grim face relaxed into a smile. "Well, ma'am, Mr. Nicholas being an active gentleman, I don't think he takes kindly to being kept in bed."

Seeing Margaret's perplexity at this conversation, Mrs. Hollis said, "Didn't you know my son had 'flu? I thought Nannie would have been sure to mention it."

"I've been too busy in the sick-room to have time for conversation," was the unexpected reply.

"I don't believe it," Mrs. Hollis laughed. "No wonder Nicholas has been like a bear with a sore head. Perhaps we'd better let Miss Grant take the magazines in to him. A bit of a diversion is called for, Nannie, don't you think?"

"Something, that's for sure," Mrs. Macgennis answered, then before Margaret could recover from her astonishment, she said, "Come along, Miss Grant dear, I'll show you which is Master Nicky's bedroom."

In a dream, Margaret found herself outside the sitting-room door and following Mrs. Macgennis down the passage. At the end door she stopped, looked round to make sure Margaret had followed her, and then knocked. Without waiting for an answer, she opened it, placed the magazines in Margaret's unwilling arms, and ushered her into the bedroom, closing the door behind her.

Margaret stood just inside the room, clutching the armful of books and rooted to the spot. A gruff, husky voice growled at her, "If that's any more poultices, inhalations, medicine or nose drops, Mac, I don't want them. Go away!"

Margaret looked round the cheery room. A chair was drawn up in front of a glowing electric fire, and she could see a figure wearing a thick dressing gown

She was so busy that it was over a week before she and on a table nearby were a variety of bottles, spoons, cups, and a steaming bowl which was filling the air with an aroma of Friar's balsam. It was so strong that Margaret coughed. Nicholas immediately turned towards the door, and she could see he was scowling ferociously.

"Oh, it's you!" said Nicholas, faint surprise sounding in his voice.

Margaret pulled herself together and advanced to the fireside.

"I've been sent with these magazines. I didn't know you were ill. I'm sorry."

"Not half as sorry as I am," he replied huskily. 'Nannie and Mother between them have me cooped here like a croupy fowl."

His tone was so bitter that Margaret chuckled involuntarily. At her laugh, his frown vanished and he looked amused.

"Since you are here, sit down and talk to me for five minutes." He waved towards a leather-topped stool. "Forgive my not rising to get it for you."

Margaret sat down on the stool facing him and still clasping the pile of magazines.

"I shouldn't stay. Your mother has a lot to do."

"Nonsense! Mother sent you, I'll wager. She won't expect you back for a minute or two. Perhaps she thinks a pretty face will cheer me up."

Margaret blushed. She looked down, speechless.

"Good heavens, girl, what have I said to offend you now?" Nicholas said. "I never knew such a touchy female. Have you never been told you were pretty before?"

The indifferent tone stung her as it usually did. She looked up quickly, the blush dying out of her cheeks.

"Often. And I wish you wouldn't always be quite so outspoken. I blushed because you made the compliment sound facetious."

"Did I now? I assure you it was said in all sincerity. Have you never looked into a mirror?"

Margaret's eyes searched his face. She didn't reply. He sat quite still in the chair, his own face expressionless.

"Can't say the same for me, can you?" he demanded suddenly. "Don't distress yourself. I know I'm an ugly so-and-so."

Margaret to her own surprise, found herself nodding in agreement with his statement. "Yes. But your face does have character."

Nicholas let out a crack of laughter. His eyes roved over her. "My goodness, you and Nannie Macgennis make a couple! Mother certainly surrounds herself with redoubtable females."

Margaret's face crumpled into a mischievous smile. "Sorry! Did that sound impertinent? It wasn't mean to be. After all, you had just said yourself you knew you weren't handsome."

At this, Nicholas laughed until the tears stood in his eyes. Down the passage, his mother listened with her head on one side to the sound of the laughter.

She was smiling when Margaret came back to her sitting-room a minute later. "Congratulations, my dear. That's the first time I've heard Nick laugh for over a week. Miles and I were very worried about him. You're a tonic I shall prescribe again."

But Nicholas Hollis must have made a rapid recovery, because three days later he came striding out of the house just as Margaret was arriving to start work. She smiled and asked him if he felt quite recovered. Nicholas, however, only gave her a very hurried, "Yes thanks," as he flagged a taxi cruising past the house. Before Margaret could close the front door he was out of sight.

Christmas was only four weeks away now, and Margaret felt she had never been so rushed. She and her mother usually gave joint presents to friends, and she was combining her lunch hour with hurried shopping expeditions and an endeavour to snatch an extra half hour at the piles of work on her desk which seemed to get bigger instead of smaller.

The cocktail party was all arranged and so far had presented no problems. The invitations had gone out and a good many people had already sent acceptances. Margaret was opening more replies one morning when Mrs. Macgennis came in with the coffee tray. She had all the look of someone with time to burn and Margaret, gazing at her laden desk, sighed inwardly.

"Thank you," she said as the tray was put down. "Feeling well today, Mrs. Macgennis?"

"Well, me dear, I'd be feelin' a good deal better if we'd not those Miln-Prescotts always in our hair."

Margaret looked up in surprise. "I've not seen them recently myself."

"Maybe not, away in here most of the day. But Miss Blanche now—well, you can only say she's a tryer an' no mistake."

"Like that, is it?" Margaret smiled. "Your Master Nicky's fatal charm at work again?"

"She's always had an eye to him, that one," Mrs. Macgennis answered. "Why, even up to the wedding day itself, wasn't she trying to cut her own sister out?"

"Sister?"

"Shure. Mrs. Nicholas was step-sister to Miss Blanche. Wasn't I after telling you all about it when first you came to work here?"

"Did you? I'd forgotten, I'm afraid. I knew they were some sort of relation, of course."

Nannie actually snorted. "Relation—well, there's relations and relations. Not that that stuck-up miss wouldn't like to be a lot closer related. Gave that poor swate sister of hers no peace after the engagement was announced. Now she's certain she can wear Master Nicky down."

She departed, still muttering to herself, while Margaret sat thinking about this latest bit of news. Now that Nannie had reminded her, she tried to recall what she had been told about the young Mrs. Hollis. She wrinkled her brows as she struggled to remember. It was all coming back to her now that Mrs. Macgennis had nudged her memory. Mrs. Miln-Prescott had remarried when her own daughter by a previous marriage was about eight years old, and had changed the child's name to that of her new husband. Blanche must have been older than her step-sister because Margaret now distinctly remembered that Mrs. Miln-Prescott often talked about her second husband's baby daughter, and how "poor darling Daddy hadn't been able to manage until he married little me!"

Margaret sat, her hands momentarily idle, thinking about the Miln-Prescotts. She wondered if Nicholas would give in and marry Blanche. Certainly, he gave no sign of favouring her in particular on those rare occasions when Margaret had seen them together. Blanche hadn't been successful with him in his youth, and now he was an assured and even cynical man, her chances wouldn't rate very high. Still, one never knew. Nicholas Hollis was an inscrutable creature. It was hopeless to hazard a guess as to his intentions.

During the next two weeks, Margaret was too busy to have time to think about the matrimonial problems or otherwise of Nicholas Hollis. Her working day seemed to consist of a mad rush to beat the clock, and when, on the rare occasions either of Mrs. Hollis's sons came in to ask her to do anything for them, she felt more frustrated at the delay this would cause in her day's work than any other emotion. She was worried too about her mother. Mrs. Grant had caught a severe cold and this hadn't cleared up as it should. In the end Margaret had insisted on her seeing the doctor.

Dr. James had attended them for many years. When he arrived he didn't seem unduly worried about Mrs. Grant's state of health. Nevertheless, he called several times and, knowing what a busy man he was, Margaret wondered if he was feeling an anxiety about her mother he was not prepared at the moment to express. The only good news they received was the arrival of Jean one evening, to tell them she was going to have another baby.

"Well, I think that's marvellous," Margaret said, "but with those scamps of yours, however will you cope?"

"Goodness knows, but I'll manage somehow. The twins will be four by the time the new infant arrives, and there's an excellent nursery school five minutes walk away from us. If Clive takes them in the mornings, it will leave me free to get on until noon. You'll see, it'll work out fine." Jean smiled. "I only hope it's a girl this time. I know Clive is dying to have a daughter to spoil."

This piece of news seemed to buck Mrs. Grant up considerably. When Margaret arrived home the next evening, it was to find she had looked out the family christening robe and was mending a small tear in the hem.

"Anticipating things a bit, aren't you, Mother?" Margaret inquired as she pulled off her hat.

"Well, it wasn't used for the twins, so I'm hoping this time my granddaughter will wear it."

Margaret smiled. "Suppose it's granddaughters. Plural! It will be the same as the last time, two into one won't go! Jean had to buy two identical romper suits for the christening. Remember?"

"I feel it will be one, not two, this time, so I'm going to be prepared," Mrs. Grant laughingly replied.

The days until the cocktail party flew past. Mrs. Willis was coming back during the afternoon and would stay with Mrs. Grant until Margaret arrived home.

After the day's work was over, Margaret checked that the flowers were all arranged, the cocktail fancies had been delivered and were satisfactory, then she returned to her office and used the time until six o'clock in getting through some of the backlog of work which had piled up. When the clock chimed the hour, she had a wash and then changed from her suit into a plain black wool frock and tiny frivolous hat. She had made this herself from two strips of black velvet and a piece of veiling, and when she was ready it put the final touch to an unobtrusive but remarkably elegant outfit. The velvet of the hat matched a narrow band of velvet binding round the neckline of the dress, and with it Margaret wore her gold ear-rings and necklace.

The dress had done duty for the two previous cocktail parties, and Margaret grimaced at her reflection in the mirror as she surveyed her "little black frock". No individuality, she thought, as she turned to the door. She was unaware of how that plain ensemble suited her colouring, or how she would make many of the women attending this evening look over-dressed.

The evening passed off successfully and Margaret was just thinking that everything had gone very smoothly, when an incident occurred which changed her opinion. She had gone to the bedroom being used as a cloakroom to get a coat for one of Mrs. Hollis's very elderly committee members, and had come upon Blanche Miln-Prescott powdering her nose in front of the mirror on the dressing table. Although Blanche could see her in the mirror, she neither turned nor spoke as Margaret searched amongst the coats lying on the bed for the one she wanted. As Margaret found the correct coat and walked to the door Blanche turned and pretended to become aware of her for the first time.

"Oh, it's you. I never can understand why Aunt Alicia

thinks it necessary to have you here for these affairs. After all, you don't do anything Mrs. Macgennis can't do as well, if not better."

As she finished speaking, she pushed past Margaret and went down the corridor, giving the latter no time to think up a reply. Margaret followed, her eyes stormy, her lips compressed. She felt a quite uncharacteristic longing to pick up the nearest object and hurl it at the arrogant figure ahead of her.

When the last guest finally left and Margaret had helped with the tidying up and was free to leave, she discovered it was raining heavily. She rang for a taxi from her office and then put on her coat, changed her thin shoes for a pair of heavy walking shoes and went into the hall to wait until the taxi arrived. Putting her small case on the table in the middle of the hall, she started to draw on her gloves. Mrs. Hollis had ordered that the house be decorated in a seasonal manner and, in addition to the magnificent flowers, the usual evergreens, holly and mistletoe had been hung on the walls and pictures.

Margaret, however, was lost in thought, wondering for perhaps the thousandth time why Blanche Miln-Prescott was always so rude to her. Her thoughts were interrupted when a key was put into the lock, and the front door swung open abruptly as Nicholas Hollis dashed in out of the rain.

He had flung his wet overcoat on to a chair and had taken out a handkerchief to dry his face and hair before he looked up and saw Margaret. He started to walk up the hall towards her, cramming the handkerchief into his breast pocket, the beginnings of a wickedly amused smile on his face.

Margaret had just put on her second glove, and she looked at him in mild astonishment.

"How nice of you to be here to welcome me, and in such an inviting position too," Nicholas remarked.

He stopped immediately in front of her and looked

58

up. Margaret's eyes followed his and to her chagrin saw she was standing beneath an enormous bunch of mistletoe.

As she made a movement to step back, Nicholas put his hands on her shoulders. Before she was aware of his intention he kissed her swiftly on the lips. As she raised her arms to push him away, his hands fell to her elbows, and holding her firmly prisoner, he kissed her a second time. But not swiftly. This time his kiss was lingering. Margaret stood completely still, her eyes closed, filled with the sensation that her legs were turning to water. She was unaware that the little cocktail hat of velvet and tulle had slipped off her head and fallen on to the carpet, making scarcely a sound as it did so. She was only aware that though she had been kissed before, it had never been like this.

As his lips left hers, she forced herself to open her eyes. Nicholas smiled his mocking smile and bowed.

"Thank you, Miss Grant. Thank you very much indeed," and before she could think of one word to say he had released her, turned and walked into the library, shutting the door firmly behind him.

Margaret clenched her fists, angry with him but angrier with herself. At that moment the door bell pealed, and she answered it to find her taxi at the kerb. All the way to the station, and home in the train, she went over the scene again and again. Her pliant attitude throughout appalled her, and she dreaded the thought of the following Monday when she would have to face Nicholas again. Why, oh, why, she thought, didn't I bite, kick, do anything but stand there like a stuffed doll? He'll think I liked it and be more insufferable than ever! But you did like it, an inner voice murmured, you liked it enormously.

Margaret sighed as she turned in the gate and opened her own front door. She would forget all about it and act as if it hadn't happened. But the following day she was reminded that even if she had forgotten about it, someone else had not. As she prepared the lunch that Saturday lunchtime, a messenger boy delivered a large square box to her. It bore the name of a well-known florist, and when she opened it, lying on a bed of beautiful spring flowers, lay her hat with a card carrying the simple inscription:

"Once again, Miss Grant, my grateful thanks," and initialled N.H.

On Monday morning, a very stern Margaret went out to catch her train. Explanations to her mother as to the sender of the flowers had not been easy, and Jean, when the matter of the florist's box and its contents had been revealed to her by Mrs. Grant, had been frankly teasing. Margaret was determined that Nicholas Hollis was going to find out that he was dealing with no starry-eyed teenager.

However, her good intentions were wasted, as during the whole of that day she saw nothing of her antagonist. Miles Hollis came in twice to ask her to do some letters, and she was kept busy by Mrs. Hollis addressing envelopes for the dozens of Christmas cards to be sent out. When she had finished these she was roped in to help sort and parcel the gifts to be sent to Mrs. Hollis's many relatives and friends. Margaret had discovered her first Christmas there that Alicia Hollis chose, wrapped and parcelled all the presents for the people of whom she was genuinely fond. Gifts for acquaintances she got one of the departmental stores to despatch. It was a distinction which amused Margaret, but, as she watched Mrs. Hollis wrapping presents for her sister, nieces, nephews and other relatives and close friends, first in mounds of tissue, followed by exquisitely figured wrapping paper and nylon ribbon, she could almost see the delighted recipients unwrapping them on Christmas morning.

Though she was not allowed to see or handle these, Margaret knew that somewhere hidden from sight would be a pile of gifts for all the other members of the household, each one individually wrapped. Even Cook's niece who came in only occasionally to help would not have been forgotten.

Mrs. Hollis's face had lost its usual air of vague detachment, and for the moment wore one of warm interest. It was obvious each gift had been selected with loving care.

She really is a dear, thought Margaret. How lucky I was to get this job. And then for a moment her thoughts stopped abruptly as she remembered Nicholas. Since his arrival, her peace of mind seemed to have completely vanished. Not all of it was due to his unpredictable ways either, her heart said. That kiss, so lightly so mockingly given last Friday had shattered all her calm. The girl who had resigned herself to a lifetime of taking care of a sick mother seemed to have vanished, and in her place was left a restless mortal whose only ambition was to pack a bag and go. To go away anywhere, to any place that would not remind her of a slight, dark, utterly bewitching man, who was laying a spell on her.

As Margaret put her coat on and picked up the pile of parcels and cards she was taking to the post office, she sighed. Spells were not for her. Rather the prosaic life of a dutiful daughter.

Three days later, returning from a lunchtime shopping spree on her own account, Margaret found Nicholas sitting in her office. She dumped her parcels on the table in the window, glad of an excuse to turn her back for an instant, and silently praying that her ever-ready flush would not betray her.

She managed to produce a cool little voice as she apologized for her late return from lunch and for keeping him waiting. "If you'll wait just a couple more minutes, Mr. Hollis, I can put these things out of the way and hang up my coat."

"Take your time. I've only been here a couple of

minutes myself and I've not yet sorted these letters and decided how I shall reply to them."

Margaret looked at him sharply as she removed her hat and coat. Usually he came into the office with what he wanted completely cut and dried, and would begin to dictate almost before she had time to pick up pencil and notebook. Could he too be remembering their last meeting with some embarrassment, or did he realize her own nervousness and was attempting to give her time to pull herself together? No, that couldn't be, she thought. She had not attempted to thank him for the flowers, and she wondered if he would think her very rude if she followed her own inclinations to ignore his gift, sent, she felt sure, in the spirit of pure devilry.

However he gave her no chance to say anything as he looked up at that moment and asked abruptly, "Ready?"

Margaret hastily picked up a shorthand notebook and slipped into the seat opposite him.

When Nicholas eventually said, "Well, I think that's the lot," Margaret looked at him directly for the first time since she had entered her office. It was to find Nicholas watching her searchingly. For a moment they stared at each other silently and then, while Margaret was wishing desperately that some easy, casual remark would spring to mind, Nicholas Hollis surprised her yet again with one of his abrupt questions.

"How old are you, Miss Grant?"

Margaret still stared in silence for a moment more before she spoke. "Twenty-six."

"Are you really?" I should have guessed twenty-one or two at the most."

Margaret smiled and said unthinkingly, "Why? Do I look so young and immature?"

She could have bitten out her tongue at her impulsive remark, but Nicholas's face remained quite expressionless. Then Margaret saw the gleam of fun begin in his eyes. "You looked both last Friday. Never been kissed before?"

She forgot the threatening blush and said sharply, "Don't be silly. Does anyone reach the age of twenty-six without having the odd flirtation?"

"Well, not usually. But I understand from Mother that you are a very devoted daughter and seldom stray far from you mamma."

Margaret looked down at her hands and then, since the subject had been broached said, "Talking of last Friday, thank you for sending my hat. The flowers were beautiful."

"I'm glad you liked them. I felt some compensation was due to you."

"Compensation?"

"Yes. You lost both your hat and your self-possession, didn't you, my dear Miss Grant?"

Nicholas was openly smiling his most mocking smile as he strolled towards the door. When it closed softly behind him, Margaret still had not found her voice.

The following week Margaret had a holiday. Christmas Day was on the Thursday and Mrs. Hollis and her family were going into the country for Christmas, so the London house would be empty since Cook too had the week off. Mrs. Grant was delighted to have Margaret at home all day, since it gave them time together to undertake one or two tiresome household mending jobs, and Margaret also took the opportunity of having a leisurely session at the hairdresser's.

Since they were to spend Christmas Day with Clive and Jean, Margaret had a big baking morning so that they would have enough pastry and cakes to last over the week-end.

She was very pleased with the re-styling which a competent hairdresser had given her. He had cut her hair much shorter and had coaxed the soft naturally wavy hair into one of the latest styles and had afterwards shown Margaret how to keep it that way herself.

When he showed her the completed coiffeur from all angles in the mirror, Margaret had to admit that the style certainly suited her. It brought out the lines of her cheekbones and drew attention to the beauty of the velvety brown eyes.

As she was hurrying to catch a bus back home, she turned into Piccadilly and bumped straight into the arms of William Pettigrew. To her surprise, he seemed unexpectedly glad to see her, and before she could protest, he had taken her arm and steered her across the road and inside a nearby teashop.

"I can't stay," Margaret protested. "I was just going to get the bus to the station. Mother is expecting me home on the four o'clock train."

"Stop and have a cup of tea. I say, you can ring your mother from here and say you've met an old friend and will be coming home later," Dr. Pettigrew suggested.

Margaret was tempted. She was pleased with her appearance, and it was a long time since any man had pressed her into deliberately playing truant. She laughed as William Pettigrew placed a threepenny piece in her hand and said, "Go on. The telephone's near the cash desk."

She returned from the phone to find a lavish tea on the table, and Dr. Pettigrew sitting waiting for her to pour.

"All okay?" he asked. "I've been kicking myself ever since the Hollis's dinner party for not asking you for your phone number, so this is my lucky day."

Afterwards he took her to the station, and before he put her into the train, had obtained a promise from her to dine with him in the near future.

On Christmas Eve, a bulky parcel arrived addressed jointly to Margaret and her mother. They guessed that it was from Mrs. Hollis, as she had always included Mrs. Grant when sending a Christmas gift. To their surprise, however, in addition to the lavish box of beribboned chocolates, and the box of nylon stockings, the parcel also contained a beautiful brown leather handbag and a pair of matching court shoes.

When Margaret dazedly tried these on, she found them a perfect fit.

"I can't understand it, Mother," Margaret said as she took the shoes off again and put them back in their tissue paper. "Mrs. Hollis always sends lovely presents, but never as expensive as this. And how on earth did she guess my size?"

Mrs. Grant stroked her hand down the sheen of the handbag before replying.

"Well, dear, I should think the son has had something to do with this. After all, you have done a lot of extra work for him. As to size, you leave an old pair of shoes in the house, don't you, for changing on rainy days?"

"Of course!" Margaret exclaimed. "But I never thought of anyone noticing."

Mrs. Grant smiled. "From what you say of him and from the brief glimpse I had at the theatre on my birthday, I shoudn't think anything escapes Nicholas Hollis."

"Whatever makes you think that, Mother? Margaret asked, her eyes curious.

"No reason in particular. It's just the estimate I've formed from listening to you speak of him. The onlooker sees a lot of the game you know, Margaret."

Margaret carefully wrapped the shoes and handbag and put them back in the box. She wondered just what her mother had implied by her last remark. Did she guess at Margaret's interest in the visitor from Rhodesia; an interest she was loth to admit even to herself?

Christmas Day proved to be much as Margaret anticipated. Clive collected them in the car after morning church, and they arrived to find Jean with the turkey and all its etceteras well under control, but knee-deep in holly wrapping paper as the twins discovered each new treasure.

They were joined for Christmas dinner by Clive's parents, and his sister, her husband and five-year-old son. It was a really jolly family party which everyone enjoyed. After lunch they played children's games until teatime, then, following a nursery tea, Margaret helped Jean bath and put the boys to bed.

Mrs. Grant also was beginning to look rather tired, so Clive got the car out and ran them home early. When her mother was warmly tucked up in bed, a hot water bottle at her feet and a light supper on a tray beside her, Margaret went back into the sitting-room.

She picked up a book, intending to read for a short time before turning in herself. Instead she found her eyes straying more and more to the gaily wrapped box containing the shoes and handbag. Had they really been purchased by Nicholas? She would have given a great deal to know.

CHAPTER FIVE

WHEN Margaret went in to work the following Monday, it was to find that Mrs. Hollis had not returned, as planned, from her Christmas holiday. There were a great many letters to be dealt with, however, and Margaret found her day fully occupied in opening and sorting correspondence, and in answering those letters which required an immediate reply.

The next morning, Miles Hollis told her that his mother would not be returning until the end of the week. Unused to the rigours of an English winter, Nicholas had caught flu again, and there was the threat of pneumonia.

Mrs. Hollis rang Margaret each morning and they

discussed over the telephone anything which was very urgent. However, as she went into her sitting-room on the first morning of her employer's return, Margaret's arms were full of letters and lists.

Mrs. Hollis laughed. "We shall be working non-stop, I can see, Margaret, for a day or two."

"Yes, I'm afraid so. We've had an exceptionally heavy post every morning," Margaret answered.

Without delay, they got down to the thousand and one matters requiring their attention, and by the end of the first week, Margaret was relieved to see her "In" basket looking a good deal emptier. It was then that Mrs. Hollis made her unexpected request. When Margaret took the letters up for signature that afternoon, she found her energetic employer for once sitting still and enjoying a solitary cup of tea.

As Margaret put the letters down beside her, Mrs. Hollis looked up. "Can you spare a minute before you go for your train?"

Margaret glanced at her. "Why, yes. I don't need to leave for another ten minutes."

"Then sit down, my dear. I've a favour to ask you."

Margaret sat down and folded her hands in her lap. She wondered what was coming.

"You know my son is getting over influenza? Well, he's not yet completely fit and Miles has persuaded him to stay down at Ashfordhurst for a little longer. He's got a lot of work on though, and unless I can get some-one to go down for a day or two and give him a hand with the clerical part, I'm afraid he'll just pack up and come to town. Now, I was wondering if you'd go down on Friday and stay until the Monday morning. That should see him through the worst."

Margaret stared. "But Mother, Mrs. Hollis . . ."

"Yes, I'd thought of that. Now is there any reason why she shouldn't go with you? A quiet week-end in the country might be a pleasant change for her."

Margaret was staggered at the suggestion.

"May I have this evening to talk it over with Mother? I'll let you know in the morning."

"By all means. I do hope she will agree. I don't want Nicholas dashing up to town until he's really well, and he will if I can't arrange something for him."

Margaret went home in a daze. It would be a lovely break for her mother, and Mrs. Hollis has promised to arrange for a hired car to take them from door to door. On the other hand, would Nicholas think her yet another female victim of his charm if she fell in so easily with this request? The memory of those kisses in the hall lingered to torment her. In all probability however, he had completely forgotten the whole episode and she was flattering herself if she thought he gave her as much as a passing thought.

When they were sitting comfortably in front of the fire that evening, cups of creamy coffee in their hands, Margaret told her mother about Mrs. Hollis's suggestion for the coming week-end. As she had guessed, Mrs. Grant immediately urged her to agree.

"So I'm to say 'yes', am I?" Margaret asked.

"By all means. When do we go?"

"Friday afternoon. But don't be too over-anxious now, Mother. It may all fall through."

But it didn't fall through and Friday saw Margaret and Mrs. Grant travelling down to Kent. When they eventually reached their destination and turned off the main road, Margaret was conscious of a feeling of disappointment. She didn't know what she had expected, but the drive bordered on either side by thick impenetrable rhododendron bushes, she thought singularly depressing. Rounding a bend, however, there, amidst green lawns, lay a beautiful, mellowed old house, sprawling in the winter sunshine. Its diamond panes glittered like a thousand eyes as the car drew nearer.

When they drew up at the three shallow steps which gave on to the wide front door, Margaret saw that this was open and that an elderly man was awaiting their arrival. As soon as the car drew to a standstill, he opened the rear door and handed Mrs. Grant out. Margaret followed her carrying her mother's bag and a rug.

As they were ushered into the hall, Margaret couldn't help a twinkle appearing in her eyes as she whispered in her mother's ear, "Is it as nice as you expected?"

Mrs. Grant in her turn smiled delightedly, and that was how Nicholas saw them as he emerged from a room at the back of the hall. Mother and daughter enjoying a private joke. His momentary hesitation as he watched them went unnoticed. Margaret was quite unconscious of his presence until he started to walk towards them. She introduced him to her mother.

"But we've already met briefly, Mrs. Grant. At the theatre. Do you remember?"

Nicholas smiled his charming smile as he steered Mrs. Grant in the direction of the staircase. "I expect you're both tired and would like a wash. Tea is ready when you are. Roberts will show you the way."

He had not spoken directly to Margaret, and only gave her a brief smile as he turned his back and went away. He doesn't look as if he's been very ill, she thought. Undoubtedly his tan was disappearing, but he looked much as usual.

She followed Roberts and her mother upstairs to the two charming bedrooms which had been prepared for them. They were separated by a bathroom, and on the other side of her mother's room was a small sitting-room with a view overlooking the gardens at the rear of the house.

Mrs. Grant walked over to the fireplace and held out her hands to the glowing electric fire, which had obviously been turned on some time previously. "Lovely, isn't it, Margaret? I shall be able to sit here and browse over a book while you and Mr. Hollis are working."

When they had freshened themselves, Margaret and Mrs. Grant went downstairs. At the foot of the staircase they found Roberts waiting to show them into the sitting-room. Tea had been set out on a small table in front of a huge fire, and as they entered the room, Nicholas Hollis rose to his feet.

"Please come and sit down. Not cold, are you?"

"No, thank you," Mrs. Grant replied, "but I must admit a cup of tea will be most welcome."

"Perhaps you'd do the honours, then," said Nicholas, and he ushered Margaret's mother towards the chair behind the tea table.

Over tea he conversed easily with Mrs. Grant, completely putting her under his spell. Margaret watched her mother talking and laughing, quite at home with this strange man, who as often as not completely ignored her, as he was doing at this moment. In fact, apart from passing her cup and the various plates of sandwiches and small cakes when her plate was empty, she might not have been there at all.

Margaret could feel her temper beginning to rise when Nicholas suddenly turned to her and said, 'Sorry to seem in such a hurry, but if you have finished tea, do you think we might press on? I've rather a lot I would like to do, and the sooner we get at it the better. You will excuse us, Mrs. Grant, won't you? Roberts has orders to look after you this afternoon and see that you're comfortable. Ask him for anything you want. Margaret and I will see you at about seven for the evening meal."

He smiled again and walked to the door, holding it open for Margaret. As if she were hypnotised, Margaret placed her cup and saucer on the table and rose. She grimaced expressively as she passed her mother. Mrs. Grant smiled mischievously. If Nicholas Hollis noticed this by-play, he made no sign, merely standing patiently holding the door open for Margaret to precede him.

Crossing the hall, he said, "Your mother will understand, I trust," and obviously not expecting a reply, he flung open a door and jerked his head for her to go into the room.

As soon as they were inside, Nicholas went to the desk and sat down beside it. Beside the desk was a small easy chair and he pushed a pad and pencil across to Margaret and nodding at the chair said, "Sit down, Miss Grant, and let's get all this done. Sorry to drag you down from town like this, but Mother explained to you, didn't she? Can't say I was pleased myself when I got this pushed into my lap."

No reply was expected, so Margaret merely smiled politely and sitting down, picked up pad and pencil.

For two hours, Nicholas dictated continuously, until Margaret began to think he was never going to stop. When he walked to the fireplace and stirred the logs with his foot, she surreptitiously rubbed her right hand. It was feeling quite cramped and she hoped that they would soon take a break.

However, half an hour later when the gong sounded through the house, Nicholas was still dictating. He jerked up his head at the sound and said incredulously, "Good heavens! Is that the time?" and looked at his watch. 'We'd better have a wash and something to eat. We can go on afterwards."

Margaret sighed. The man wasn't human! As she rose he said:

"Be quick, won't you? Supper will be ready in fifteen minutes."

Margaret carefully put the pad and pencil on the desk and walked quietly out of the room without speaking It was as much as she could do not to burst into indignant speech. When she reached the door, something made her look back. Nicholas was sitting watching her, and as she caught his eye, she could have sworn he was trying not to laugh. Her indignation rose as she walked

71

upstairs. Odious man! She was so deep in her indignant thoughts that she nearly walked into her mother, who was coming along the corridor towards her.

"There you are, my dear. I think supper is ready."

"In fifteen minutes, Mother. Come and sit in my room while I wash."

Mrs. Grant sat on the bed while Margaret pulled her jumper over her head and went into the bathroom for a hasty wash. As she ran the water she called, "Had a terribly boring afternoon, Mother?"

"No, quite the contrary. Roberts and I found we had one or two subjects in common, and in the end he unbent sufficiently to show me round the house, ending in the kitchen where he introduced me to his wife. Do you know, the two of them look after the house entirely on their own. Mrs. Roberts does all the cooking too, they have no outside help. They're real workers, nothing seems to be too much trouble. She even asked me to let her know if I have any favourite dishes I fancy. Wasn't that kind of her?"

Margaret laughed through the folds of the towel which she was busily using. "Honestly, Mother, you're priceless! How do you manage to get round people so easily? I can never do it. You'll have to tell me your secret some time."

She walked over to her suitcase as she spoke, and got out a lighter blue woolen top, which toned perfectly with her skirt. She pulled it on and then quickly started to re-do her face, lightly touching her eyebrows and eyelashes with mascara and settling her hair into its new soft style. She fastened a simple string of inexpensive pearls round her throat as she turned and asked, "Will I do?"

"Very nice, dear. Come along, I believe I'm hungry."

"Good!" Margaret said as she tucked her hands in her mother's arm.

Roberts was again waiting at the foot of the stairs. "I think Mr. Nicholas would like you to have a sherry before your supper, Madam," and as he spoke he threw open the sitting-room door.

Nicholas Hollis was standing in front of the fire, a glass in one hand and some papers in the other. He was frowning, but as he saw them come in, he walked over and threw the papers down and moved a chair closer to the fire.

"Come and sit down, Mrs. Grant. What shall I get you to drink? Sherry? Or would you prefer something else?"

"Sherry will do very nicely," Mrs. Grant replied. "Margaret and I both like it dry if you've got it, please."

Nicholas poured out two glasses of wine from one of the bottles on a wagonette against the wall and brought them over. Margaret was leaning against the arm of her mother's chair, but she straightened up as he placed the glass in her hand, and their eyes met. He bowed very slightly, the old mocking light appearing in his eyes as they ran over her. To her disgust, Margaret felt herself colouring, and to cover her embarrassment, rushed into speech.

"Mother has been making herself thoroughly at home. She's even invaded the kitchen and made the acquaintance of your Mrs. Roberts."

"Have you?" Nicholas sounded surprised. "You're honoured indeed if Roberts has taken you to see his missus. They've both been here since Miles and I were small and are a law unto themselves. They soon make it obvious if some of our visitors don't measure up to their standards, and it can be a nuisance. I've told Mother she should get rid of them, but I doubt if she could. They're practically an institution."

"Oh, you mustn't do that, ever." Mrs. Grant sounded quite shocked. "Mrs. Roberts is quite wonderful. I didn't think people of her calibre still existed."

Nicholas laughed. "Yes, but sometimes she can be very tiresome, you know."

He walked over and refilled his glass as he spoke. Margaret, who hadn't thought he looked particularly ill when she arrived, suddenly noticed that his face looked drawn and thinner than she remembered. As if he noticed her scrutiny, Nicholas frowned, the black eyebrows drawing together into one thick bar. He downed his drink in one gulp and said, "If you've finished your drink, Mrs. Grant, we'll eat."

Mrs. Grant gave him her empty glass and rose to her feet. Nicholas offered her his arm and led her out, Margaret following them, carrying her mother's handbag. Roberts was waiting in the dining-room, and as soon as they were seated began to serve the meal.

The soup was hot and tasty, and it was followed by a roast duck, accompanied to Margaret's secret relief by the old-fashioned sage and onion stuffing, apple sauce, peas and small delicately roasted potatoes. She had never liked orange with duck, and knew that her mother shared this dislike.

As if she sensed Margaret's thoughts, Mrs. Grant smiled across the table at her daughter. Nicholas seated between them at the head of the table intercepted the look and raised his brows quizzically.

"We don't like duck and orange, Margaret and I," explained Mrs. Grant. "We were so relieved to see it served this way we were signalling our satisfaction to each other."

Nicholas laughed. "I couldn't agree more. If Mrs. Roberts had cooked a duck with orange when I was here, it really would have been more than her job was worth."

They all laughed at the tone of his voice.

When the sweet and savoury had been served, Nicholas said, "I wonder if you'd mind if Margaret and I disappeared for a moment, Mrs. Grant? Roberts will be bringing coffee, and I understand there's a good play on the television this evening."

"Now don't bother about me, Mr. Hollis," said Mrs. Grant. "I shall be perfectly content to entertain myself until bedtime."

Margaret followed Nicholas back to the room he was using as a temporary office. When she turned from shutting the door behind her, he was already lifting a typewriter on to a small table which had been put beside the bigger desk.

"Will you be all right here? Sorry to be such a slave driver, but if you could do a draft of what I've dictated so far, then I could check it tonight after you've gone to bed."

Margaret opened her mouth, "But you've . . ." she had been going to say, "Shouldn't you have early nights when you have been so ill?" but the look on Nicholas's face had stopped her in mid-sentence.

His voice was at its most cold and indifferent as he said, "Will you mind starting right away, please?"

It was more an order than a request, and Margaret sat down and pulled the typewriter towards her with a mutinous face. As she inserted a piece of paper into the machine, she glared across at the man already unzipping the briefcase he had laid on the desk. To her surprise he glanced up and seeing the look in Margaret's eyes, said in a soft drawl, "Always remember, Meg, I hate solicitious women."

Margaret opened her mouth and then closed it again sharply. How had he guessed she had been about to make some comment on his recent ill health? Her face must be amazingly revealing. And calling her "Meg" too, she thought, as she looked down at the first line of shorthand in her book. It was a hateful nickname, one she had never allowed anyone to use. But she had to admit in that deep, soft voice, it had sounded delightful. She had once heard Nat King Cole's voice described as being like treacle poured out of a tin. The description here too was apt!

You stupid idiot, she told herself. Get on with your work and forget the man!

She typed on steadily, and by her right hand the pile of finished pages grew. She was unaware when Nicholas rose quietly to his feet and left the room. Unaware when two hours later he returned with a tray in his hand. It was not until the jingle of crockery penetrated her consciousness that her hands stilled over the typewriter keys, and she looked up.

The clock over the mantelpiece said ten-thirty. She had had no idea that time had gone so quickly.

"Your mother has just gone up to bed. Have a hot drink, then perhaps you'd like to go too. You've had a long day."

Margaret flipped over the pages of her notebook. "I've only one more page after this. If you don't mind, I'd prefer to finish it."

"By all means, if you wish," Nicholas said indifferently, and he turned away to pour out the coffee. Taking one of the cups across to the fire, he returned to Margaret and picked up the pile of finished work. He flung himself into a fireside chair and started to read it through.

Margaret quickly finished the rest of the draft, and took the remaining pages across to him. She placed them on the arm of Nicholas's chair, but received only a grunt of acknowledgement. She turned away without saying goodnight, and picking up her cup of coffee, carried it across the room and up the stairs to her mother's bedroom.

Mrs. Grant was sitting comfortably in bed, reading by the light of a soft, rose-shaded bedside lamp. She had a small tray beside her containing a plate of biscuits and a beaker of hot chocolate. She smiled as she saw Margaret and said, "Finished, dear?" Margaret nodded. "Nicholas has been most kind to me this evening," Mrs. Grant went on.

"Nicholas?" exclaimed Margaret, surprise in her voice.

"Yes. He told me Mr. Hollis sounded too formal. He came back into the sitting-room soon after you started typing, and stayed to watch the play with me. Poor boy,

I think he was a bit bored with it. Not a man's play at all."

Mrs. Grant gave her gurgling laugh. "Still, he was very polite and put on a good front. In fact I think he deserves a medal for being so kind to a dull old woman, and one he hardly knows too."

"Don't be silly, Mother," said Margaret. "Nicholas Hollis in never polite, I'm sure, without a motive. After all, he's getting his typing done, so it won't hurt him to behave decently to the typist's mother. Who else would come down from London at such short notice and work half the night?"

Since she didn't expect an answer, Margaret was surprised when her mother said, "Well, maybe. But not everyone would bother. I think he's a very nice boy, but he looks ill and sad."

"Sad?" Margaret's voice soared to a squeak in her astonishment. "Don't you mean plain bad-tempered?"

Her mother merely smiled and shook her head. "I think you're so prejudiced you never really look at him, my dear. Try it some time. It might change your opinion."

"Never," Margaret said definitely. "He's the coldest, most cynical individual I've ever encountered." But as she tucked her mother in and kissed her good night, she wondered if she were speaking to convince herself or Mrs. Grant. A cynic, Nicholas might be, but that didn't alter the fact that she found his presence stimulating. Even when he made her tremble with rage, there was still that appeal. Yes, Margaret thought to herself, it's that damnable appeal which is the trouble. How I hate the fact that he can absorb my thoughts and interest so much!

Something inside her laughed at the thought that she had presumed herself to be immune to this virile, challenging man. Had presumed she would be different and not follow irresistibly in the wake of all the other women who found him so attractive. I'll be different, though, she promised herself. Whatever my feelings, I shall hide them. I won't make a fool of myself as Mrs. Macgennis says so many others have done.

The following morning, she left her mother breakfasting in bed and went downstairs at eight-thirty to find Nicholas Hollis already in the dining-room. He rose as she came in and pulled out a chair.

"What will you have, Miss Grant? There's bacon and one or two other things on the hot plate there. We always help ourselves at breakfast time."

"Thanks, just coffee and toast, please."

As he poured out a cup of coffee and passed it to her Nicholas said, "Slimming? I shouldn't have thought it necessary."

He glanced meaningly up and down her, an impish smile in his eyes.

Despite herself, Margaret coloured. "Must you always make embarrassing remarks to me?" she exclaimed sharply before she could stop herself. Then she flushed even more hotly and bit her lip.

Nicholas looked at her for a moment in silence before bursting into a hearty chuckle. "Sorry, my dear. Don't mind me. Eat what you like."

Against her better judgment, Margaret found herself smiling. "Thank you, I will," and she selected a piece of toast and began to butter it.

Margaret spent most of that day shut up in the room Nicholas used as an office. They worked together all that morning, then in the afternoon, while Margaret typed on alone, he took Mrs. Grant for a run down to the sea.

On their return, he continued working with Margaret while her mother had a rest. At nine o'clock on Saturday evening, Margaret was sent out to have a break from work. Though she would have quite willingly gone straight to bed, she sat through a television programme in the sitting-room to keep her mother company.

Sunday morning, Margaret managed to get in two hours in the office before she had to get ready to accompany Mrs. Grant to morning service in the little village church. The choir of well-scrubbed country boys was surprisingly good, and Margaret enjoyed the anthem which followed the second lesson. As she sat listening to the clear young voices, and looking at the beautiful stained-glass window over the altar, the tiredness caused by the gruelling amount of work she had got through since Friday fell away from her, as did the inner conflict she was waging almost subconsciously against the attraction she felt for Nicholas Hollis. She sighed when the singing ended and returned to following the service almost reluctantly.

Despite a cold wind, the sun was shining brightly when they came out of church to find the car waiting for them at the gate. To Margaret's astonishment, Nicholas was behind the wheel.

"We'll have a run before lunch," he said as he got out to help them into the car. "It will give us all a breath of fresh air."

Later that afternoon, when Nicholas was revising two pages of the report and Margaret was sitting waiting for his instructions, they both heard the front doorbell ring. Nicholas raised his head and swore quietly under his breath.

Voices could be heard in the hall, Robert's obviously raised in protest, when the door was flung open and Blanche Miln-Prescott came into the room.

"Nicholas darling! Why ever didn't you let us know you were still down here? I'm staying with the Websters over at Kenner, and Mildred said she saw you outside church this morning. You must come to dinner tonight. Now don't tell me you're too busy or anything."

"Sorry, Blanche," said Nicholas when at last she paused, "but I'm afraid I am. Tell the Websters I'm most grateful for their invitation, but really I am up to my ears in work."

"Nonsense! You can leave it for one evening, darling. We'll expect you at eight o'clock, then."

The discussion was rapidly developing into an argument, and Margaret got up and started to walk quietly towards the door. Nicholas's brows immediately met in a frown.

"Don't go, Miss Grant. I want to get on with this. Sorry, Blanche, but I really must ask you to excuse me."

He started to guide Blanche towards the door, his hand at her elbow. She pulled her arm abruptly out of his hand and swung on Margaret.

"And what is the obsequious Miss Grant doing down here? Is she the only person capable of pounding a typewriter in the whole of London?"

Nicholas looked long suffering. He stopped in the middle of the room, his brows raised.

"You always did become vulgar and personal when you couldn't get your own way, didn't you, Blanche? I see you don't change with the years."

The virago of a moment before underwent an immediate metamorphosis. Blanche turned, smiled and walking towards Nicholas laid her hand gently on his arm.

"Darling, don't let's say anything we'd be sorry for afterwards." The tones were sickly-sweet. "Drop all this horrid old work and come and see little Blanche this evening."

Margaret felt faintly sick. She didn't know which she disliked more, Blanche Miln-Prescott showing her claws or behaving in this sickly little-girl manner. One was as bad as the other. What Nicholas was thinking she couldn't guess. He looked at Blanche with his customary bored, indifferent smile, and merely opened the door and bowed her out.

What was said at the other side of the solid oak door

Margaret couldn't have heard had she tried. Instead she sat down at the typewriter and typed two or three lines without having the slightest idea of what she was reading from her shorthand notebook. Her thoughts were on the scene she had just unwillingly witnessed.

Five minutes later she heard the front door slam. Immediately the library door opened with a snap and Nicholas walked back into the room. His face looked thunderous as he went straight to the tray of bottles and poured himself a large whisky, which he drank in one gulp. He poured a second drink and took it across to the fire, still without saying a word. Sitting down, he sat for several minutes staring into the fire.

Margaret peeped at him once briefly through her lashes, then, seeing he looked remarkably stern, she started to transcribe her notes in earnest.

It must have been quite fifteen or twenty minutes later when Nicholas got up abruptly and put his empty glass on the mantelpiece. "Shall we continue, Miss Grant?" and without waiting for a reply, he said, "Please read out my last sentence."

Margaret complied. The afternoon wore away and with it the report Nicholas was doing neared completion.

"I think that's enough until after supper," he remarked. "We'll do the last-minute alterations then and, thank heaven, I think it should be satisfactory. Perhaps you'd like to go and rest now. Supper ought to be ready in about half an hour."

Margaret put her pencils and papers away and went upstairs. Mrs. Grant was reclining on an old-fashioned but comfortable-looking day-bed in the small sitting-room next door to her bedroom, a book in her hands. She looked up and smiled when she saw her daughter.

"Tired, Margaret? It's been a busman's week-end for you. I expect you're sick of the sight of a typewriter. Sit down and relax for a few minutes. You'll still have time for a quick bath before supper."

Margaret was very glad to do as her mother suggested.

She did indeed feel tired. Her shoulders ached and she felt unreasonably depressed. That it might be due to the intrusion of Blanche Miln-Prescott she did not admit to herself. There was no doubt, however, that her visit had caused Nicholas to behave like a bear with a sore head. For the remainder of the afternoon he had been abrupt and taciturn. He'd also replenished his whisky glass on several occasions and when, after a soothing bath and a change into a soft green woollen dress, Margaret went down with her mother for their pre-supper sherry, it was to find him still drinking.

During the evening meal, however, he had only one glass of wine and was obviously making an effort to put aside the black mood he was feeling. He apologized to Mrs. Grant for not being able to take her out during the afternoon, and laughed when she admitted that she had actually slept from lunchtime until tea had been brought in to her.

"I enjoyed it just as much as a trip into the country-side believe me," she said, her eyes twinkling, and Margaret was secretly relieved to see Nicholas relax and laugh in return.

"Yes, I must admit there's nothing like a good, sound sleep Sunday afternoon," he agreed. "It's one of the compensations of middle age."

"Middle age—poof!" replied Mrs Grant. "You're only a bit of a lad yet."

Nicholas smiled widely at this remark. "Thank you, ma'am. I'll have you know, however, I'm rapidly reaching the sere and yellow."

"Well, you'll be a year or two yet before you feel that a nap is preferable to going out," was all she replied.

When they had finished coffee, Nicholas raised his brows and, guessing his unspoken question, Margaret at once got up.

"You'd like to do the corrections now, I expect, Mr. Hollis."

"Yes. Sorry to be such a hard taskmaster, but I want the damn thing finished and done with. You'll excuse us yet again, won't you, Mrs. Grant?"

Nicholas and Margaret went into the cosy room on the other side of the hall and settled down to work once more. To Margaret's relief, there were very few alterations necessary, and these were of a minor nature. It was only just after nine o'clock when she handed the finished work across the desk to Nicholas. In return he put a sealed envelope into her hand.

"A small remuneration for all your work," he said as he picked up the report and started to leaf through it.

Margaret thanked him and then tidied her table. When she had done so, she opened the envelope and a cheque for twenty-five pounds fell out.

Before she could think coherently, she said, "But I can't accept this."

Nicholas's head jerked up. "Why ever not? You've worked hard and earned every penny of it."

"I still can't take all this." Margaret stood there, the picture of embarrassment, holding the cheque out towards him.

"Nonsense! Put it in your handbag. It will help towards your next new hat."

Margaret stood her ground. She summoned all her courage and said, "I mean it, Mr. Hollis. This is far too much. I've only worked two days here, and the very most I'll accept is ten pounds."

Nicholas looked up and studied her thoughtfully. Margaret put the cheque on the desk in front of him, and stepped back. Her mouth felt dry and she wished, for the hundredth time, that circumstances did not compel her to be so careful with what little spare money she had. How nice it would have been to have felt free to brush aside any question of payment completely, but ten pounds would go quite a way to buying the extras which Mrs. Grant needed, and which their combined incomes scarcely covered.

She turned away and was going towards the door, when his voice arrested her. "Just a moment. If you won't accept this cheque as it stands, how about my purchasing an hour of your company this evening for the extra fifteen pounds? One hour in which you would do exactly as I requested. Now think. If you refuse your mother won't get that week-end by the sea you promised her."

Margaret turned and her eyes opened wide. So did her mouth, with complete astonishment. How had he known that she pinched and scraped every additional penny she could lay her hands on in order that her mother could go to Bournemouth occasionally? She supposed, knowing her mother, that many confidences had been told on those occasions when Nicholas had left Margaret to work here alone and had gone away to entertain Mrs. Grant by himself.

Her face flamed again with embarrassment as she thought of what those confidences might involve. Margaret was essentially proud, and the thought that her mother might have told Nicholas just how difficult they found it to make ends meet left her speechless.

"Well, what do you say?"

"It's ridiculous! Fifteen pounds for one hour? And what should I have to do?"

"That, my dear girl, you'd have to wait and find out. Now is it a deal? Look, it's now nine-fifteen. Go up— see your mother. Say good night and come down prompt at ten o'clock. Then from ten to eleven o'clock you are at my disposal."

Margaret looked at him thoughtfully. Nicholas gave no indication of the fact that he had had several whiskies during the afternoon, but she wondered if he might be drunk. As if he recognized the way her thoughts were turning, he smiled mockingly.

"Oh no, my dear, don't imagine I'm inebriated. I'm perfectly sober, I assure you. I'd like an hour of your

84

company and that's all. Are you game? In return you will accept this cheque as it stands."

Margaret made up her mind suddenly. Aften all, it appeared silly to refuse, and the money, she admitted to herself, would be very useful.

"Very well, I'll go up now and see Mother is all right, and at ten o'clock I'll come down again for an hour."

Nicholas turned back to his papers immediately as if he had already lost interest in the whole discussion. "Until later, then," he murmured.

Margaret went upstairs and found her mother getting ready for bed. When Mrs. Grant was comfortably settled, Margaret sat beside the bed and talked. Her mother was sipping a glass of warm milk, thoughtfully provided by Mrs. Roberts.

"Well, Mother, are you sorry the week-end is over, or has it been terribly dull for you?"

"I've loved every minute of it. The house is very comfortable, and your Mr. Hollis, as well as Roberts and his wife, have been most kind."

Margaret got up, laughing as she did so. "Not so much of the 'my Mr. Hollis', please, Mother. He belongs to no one but himself."

She busied herself tidying up one or two of the garments lying about the room, putting those Mrs. Grant wouldn't require in the bottom of the suitcase.

"Did he tell you what time we're starting back tomorrow by the way?" Margaret inquired.

"No, he didn't," replied Mrs. Grant. "But it's only early. Why don't you go down now and ask him?"

Margaret could feel the blood creeping up her cheeks. For some reason she didn't feel like telling her mother about the financial arrangement with Nicholas Hollis, and she mumbled something unintelligible as she packed a spare pair of shoes down the sides of the suitcase.

Apparently Mrs. Grant noticed nothing unusual in

Margaret's demeanour, because she said, "Run away now, dear. I'm just going to read one chapter and then I think I'll be ready to nod off. I'm beginning to feel sleepy already."

Margaret kissed her cheek and then walked to the door to turn off the main light, leaving her mother to read by the light of the bedside lamp. She went into her own room and nervously powdered her nose. She dreaded the thought of the return downstairs, and wished she hadn't agreed to so extraordinary a plan.

However, when the little clock on the mantelpiece chimed ten, she screwed up her courage and walked along the corridor and down the stairs. In her nervousness, she found herself knocking almost timidly at the door. It was opened immediately, and she found herself staring into the eyes of Nicholas Hollis. But a Nicholas Hollis she had never met before. Gone was the businesslike manner with which he usually treated her, and he was levelling at her the charming smile she had seen him turn on others, but rarely on herself. To her astonishment he put out his hand and pulled her over the threshold.

"Come on in, Meg. I've been waiting for you. You're two minutes late."

Margaret was even more dumbfounded than ever, and allowed herself to be propelled to the fireside in silence. Gone were all the evidences of their busy weekend. The typewriter had disappeared, as had all the welter of papers on the big desk. It contained nothing now except a bowl of flowers and a tray of drinks. A settee had been pulled up before the roaring log fire, and Margaret found herself sitting in one corner of it. Having seen her comfortably seated, Nicholas walked over and poured drinks into two small tankards. He added ice and then strolled back to the fire and gave one to Margaret with a "Try that!"

Margaret looked suspiciously at the frosted tankard in her hand, then lifted it cautiously to her lips.

"Good heavens, girl, it's not poisoned! Drink it. It's only Pimms. Don't you like it?"

Margaret nodded. "Oh yes, thank you."

'Spoken like a good, well-mannered little girl. Come on, Meg, we're out of school tonight, so relax."

Nicholas flung himself into the other corner of the settee as he spoke and stretched out his legs. He began to talk about Africa and his home there.

Margaret was thinking how exciting it must be to travel when he remarked, "Shan't stay there for ever, of course. Mother wants me to sell up and come home for good. She never did cotton on to the idea of me living so far away. Still, I like it, and at the time I wanted to get away from England. I'd just lost Julie."

He stopped and peered into his drink as if he were seeing pictures there. It was the first time he'd mentioned his dead wife in Margaret's hearing, and she was amazed.

"You must have missed her very much."

He flung up his head and smiled, a half sad, half wistful smile.

"Sorry to become reminiscent. Have you ever been abroad?"

"Only once to France with the school, and once for a holiday with Mother and Father to Switzerland when I was little. Is Rhodesia a beautiful country? I'd love to see some of the national parks. I believe they're wonderful."

Margaret suddenly found she had lost her shyness. Nicholas seemed to have become a different person as he talked. He began to tell her details of life in Africa, and about some of the safaris he had made.

"You'd have liked one I made with some of those geographical chaps if you're interested in the unusual. They were doing a survey for some society or other. Anyway we went right up the borders of Uganda to the Ruwenzori. Have you heard of it?" Margaret shook her head. "It's called the Mountains of the Moon. Eerie place. Hardly any people live there, and the flora are quite something. Giant groundsels and lobelias hundreds of feet high. Like things on space planets in the children's comics."

He got up as he finished speaking and took the tankard out of Margaret's hand. While he had been talking she had finished its contents.

"No more for me, please," she said as he began to refill it.

"Don't be silly, Meg. You'll not get drunk on this. Are you afraid of saying something you shouldn't?"

Nicholas sat down again and handed her the drink. In his eyes was the old mocking smile, and she felt her nervousness returning.

"Come on, drink up!"

To cover her shyness, she took a small sip.

"That's my girl! We'll make a toper of you yet."

"Don't be ridiculous," said Margaret, laughing in her turn. "You make me sound like a Salvation Army lassie out on the spree. In point of fact I'm an old, experienced spinster."

As soon as the words were out, Margaret realized how silly they sounded, and it didn't need Nicholas's immediate "Are you indeed?" to bring the blood flowing to her cheeks again. Oh, her wretched habit of blushing! How she wished she had managed to control it. Nicholas watched the colour flooding into her face with a maddening smile on his mouth.

"You look delicious when you blush. Did you know?"

Margaret buried her face in her tankard, took too large a gulp, and choked. The drink was quickly taken out of her hand, put safely down, and a handkerchief handed to her.

As she wiped her streaming eyes, a hand patted her firmly between the shoulder blades. "Shame on you, Meg. I thought you just told me you were a big girl now."

Margaret woke up to the fact that the hand which had patted her back was now firmly round her, and that the handkerchief had been retrieved. Nicholas tipped up her face and wiped both her eyes very carefully. Then he slowly returned the handkerchief to his breast pocket and leaned forward casually. Margaret sat as though hypnotised as he kissed her right on the mouth. She, who drank so little, had taken sufficient alcohol this evening to make her reflexes slow, and before she could, had she wished, held Nicholas at arm's length, he had kissed her again.

This time he gathered her right into his arms, and planted a slow, deliberate kiss on her parted lips. Margaret had just time to think "this can't be me" when almost unconsciously one arm slid round his shoulder, and her fingers buried themselves in the short hair at the nape of his neck. It was surprisingly silky, and Margaret moved one finger up and down exploratively.

Nicholas drew away from her, laughing. "This wasn't my idea when I suggested you should give me an hour of your time, but I can't think of a better way to spend our last five minutes, can you?" and he kissed her again.

Margaret opened her eyes, and pushed him away. She glanced quickly at the clock on the mantelpiece. It said three minutes to eleven.

"You've only three minutes left," she said primly.

Nicholas lay back in the corner of the settee.

"Five, my dear, you arrived two minutes late. Remember? And I like you better when you let your hair down than with this prunes and prisms attitude. You can't fool me now. I've seen you when you forgot your inhibitions. You're quite something, believe me, and I know what I'm talking about."

Margaret's lips tightened. "I'm sure you do."

"Oho! She has claws too. Now I really know you're human. Before you were like an efficient, well-behaved

89

machine. Apart from one night in December, that is. I began to wonder then if you might not have hidden depths."

Margaret sprang to her feet. "Oh, you're impossible! I wish I'd never agreed to this ridiculous hour."

Nicholas got up lazily. "Two minutes to kiss me good night. You've made me feel a new man again."

Margaret glared and walked towards the door. As she passed him he shot out a hand and pulled her round into his arms. She started to struggle but, to her surprise, he controlled her without effort, pinning her arms to her sides. He forced up her chin and said softly, "Don't spoil it, Meg. I really enjoyed your company this evening. Please will you let me kiss you good night?"

Margaret eyed him thoughtfully. He looked neither mocking nor arrogant at this moment. In fact, for one instant she thought she had detected an appeal in his eyes. She stopped struggling and, without speaking, held up her mouth.

Nicholas kissed her once gently, then released her. He walked over and opened the door and, as she passed him, put the cheque into her hand. As Margaret walked into the hall, a soft "good night, Meg" followed her before the door clicked shut.

CHAPTER SIX

WHEN she reached her bedroom, Margaret switched on all the lights and walked to the mirror. Apart from a high colour in her cheeks, she looked no different than usual. The eyes in the mirror looked faintly ashamed though as the thoughts jostled one another in her head.

Of course Nicholas had just been amusing himself. But if only, she thought, he had been in earnest. She knew now only too well what Mrs. Macgennis had meant when she had said "the laddie could charm the birds out of the bushes". Despite all her prejudices, Margaret's defences had gone down headlong under the onslaught of his appeal. She found it a relief to be honest with herself at last, and probably in consequence of this, slept much better than she had anticipated.

Next morning, Mrs. Robetrs herself wakened Margaret with a breakfast tray containing grapefruit, a rack of crisp toast, butter, honey and a pot of steaming coffee.

"My goodness, Mrs. Roberts, that does look good. But am I late?" and she looked quickly at her wrist watch.

"No, it's early, miss, but Mr. Nicholas sends his compliments and says can you be ready to leave by a quarter to nine, please."

"Of course," Margaret replied, but Mother . . ."

"That's all right. She's begun her breakfast, and I'm just going now to see her packing."

Margaret smiled thankfully. "You are good, Mrs. Roberts. I can't thank you enough."

It was obvious that Mrs. Roberts was pleased. She straightened the curtains and quite unnecessarily tidied two ornaments on the dressing table before hurrying out of the room.

Margaret grinned to herself as she ate her breakfast. She finished it quickly, then, putting the tray aside, she carried her second cup of coffee into the bathroom. She had a quick bath, dressed and went along to her mother's room.

She found her mother up and dressed. She was just putting the finishing touches to her hair. "Hello, darling! I think we'd better go down right away, don't you?"

"Yes, if you're ready, Mother," Margaret replied. "I

see your packing is done. I've just got to put in my slippers and one or two other things and I'll be ready too."

A few minutes later they went downstairs together. In the hall, to Margaret's surprise, they met Nicholas, wearing a thick overcoat. The car was already at the door, and he helped Margaret and Mrs. Grant into the back before taking his place in the driving seat.

Beyond a "good morning", extended impartially to both mother and daughter, he had not spoken, and while Margaret was puzzling over this turn of events, her mother spoke.

"I didn't know Nicholas was driving us back this morning," she said in an undertone. "I thought he was supposed to be staying on because of his illness."

Margaret could not help hoping that this sudden decision might not have something to do with the events of last night, but Nicholas had paid her no special attention this morning. Indeed as the morning wore on, the events of the previous evening seemed to Margaret to become more and more like some fanciful dream. Even when they had handed over her mother to the care of a welcoming Mrs. Willis and Margaret had joined Nicholas in the front of the car for the remainder of the journey, he still behaved in the old indifferent manner, and Margaret's spirits sank more and more as the minutes passed. Just at the last, as he handed her out of the car, she chanced to see him looking at her with what she thought was the suspicion of a twinkle in his eyes, and this had the inevitable result of bringing the blood to her face. It didn't help to have Mrs. Macgennis say as she opened the door, "The week-end seems to have done you good, if I may say so. You've quite a country bloom in your cheeks, Miss Grant."

It was three weeks before she saw Nicholas Hollis again. As soon as his business had been completed in

London, he had gone to join friends in Scotland. Margaret would not admit to herself that the weeks seemed like years, and to try and counteract the depression she felt, flung herself into an orgy of work at home.

Much to Mrs. Grant's disgust, she decided to spring-clean and then redecorate the kitchen. It had previously been blue, and as it faced north it made it look rather cold. Margaret had chosen a pretty washable wallpaper in white with huge yellow roses strewn all over it. She painted the woodwork white, and bought yellow towelling to make new curtains. It took her a fortnight working in the evening and at the week-ends to complete the transformation, and by that time Mrs. Grant was threatening to leave and go and stay with Jean until it was finished.

"Goodness, Margaret, I thought you'd have left it until the spring at least. Either Mrs. Willis and I are overcome by the smell of fresh paint, or we have to have a window open and nearly freeze to death."

Margaret laughed. "Oh, Mother darling, it's not as bad as that! You know you always say the smell of paint is so clean and nice. Anyway you'll love it when it's done. I only wish we could replace the lino, but I'm afraid it will have to do for another year or two yet."

Mrs. Grant did indeed seem pleased when the kitchen was finished, and Jean, who had brought her two boisterous twins to tea, was most envious of the colour scheme. "Now, why didn't I think of yellow and white when Clive suggested doing the kitchen last year? I had it in red and pale blue, as you know, and now I don't really like it one bit. When we decorate next time, I shall definitely copy you. And aren't the curtains lovely? I only think of towelling when it comes to bathrooms, but it looks gorgeous against that wallpaper, and you clever girl, you've matched the yellow of the roses exactly."

Margaret thought that in one way her efforts had not been in vain, though working on the kitchen had not kept her thoughts in check. Night after night, as she had papered and painted, they had gone round and round in her mind. Though thoroughly tired out with all the unaccustomed exercise, she hadn't been sleeping well. On more than one occasion, she had had to get up and take an aspirin before sleep had come, and in the mornings she had felt heavy-eyed and listless. To her relief, however, neither her mother nor Mrs. Hollis seemed to notice anything untoward in her manner, and she told herself that she would get over her foolish infatuation for Nicholas if it were the last thing she did.

Consequently, when Dr. Pettigrew telephoned her one evening and invited her to have dinner with him, she accepted.

Since Mrs. Willis was unable to come and sit with Mrs. Grant that evening, Jean drove over to keep her mother company. They both teased Margaret as she got ready to leave. By the time she left to catch her train, she too was laughing. "You'd think William Pettigrew was Prince Charming and I was leaving to go to the ball, the way you two are carrying on!"

"Well, you must admit," Jean replied, "It's sufficiently unusual for you to go out at all to warrant comment. I can't remember when you last accepted a date, though you've refused a good many, I'm sure. He must have some hidden allure."

Margaret was still chuckling as she closed the garden gate behind her, and perhaps because she had set out in such good spirits, enjoyed the evening. True, they only had dinner in a quiet restaurant and talked, but she discovered Dr. Pettigrew to be an able conversationalist, and when he found she was an interested, appreciative listener, he needed no further encouragement to do most of the talking. As Margaret sat there listening to endless anecdotes of his schooldays, his time in medical school, she had to fight to keep her thoughts from wandering. Where was Nicholas at this particular

94

moment? she wondered. Who was he with, and what was *he* talking about?

However, Dr. Pettigrew did not seem to notice any lack of interest in Margaret's face, and when he finally said good night his parting words were, "We must do this again some time."

When the object of her most private thoughts entered the office a few days later in the wake of a large bouquet of flowers from William Pettigrew, his temper did not seem to have improved during his visit to Scotland. Nicholas was frowning alarmingly as Mrs. Macgennis handed the flowers to Margaret. "Floral tributes, Miss Grant! Someone obviously believes in doing things in a big way," and he waved somewhat contemptuously towards the truly enormous sheaf of flowers which Margaret was holding.

"Yes, there are rather a lot. Will you excuse me while I put them in water?" and without waiting for a reply, Margaret thankfully escaped.

When she returned five minutes later, Nicholas was sitting at her desk, calmly reading the letter which she had been typing. Wiser now where he was concerned, Margaret thought it more tactful not to comment. Almost as if he had read her thoughts, Nicholas got up and said mockingly, "What, no strictures on the ill manners of reading other people's letters? The soul of diplomacy too, are you, Miss Grant?"

Margaret knew he was deliberately provoking her, but as she walked towards her chair and sat down, she had the greatest difficulty in restraining herself.

"Admirable," Nicholas remarked. "I've always longed to meet a woman with a really remarkable self-control. You have my vote for 'Miss Golden Silence' of this year," and he lifted her hand and kissed her fingers.

Margaret looked up, and as he released her hand, she whipped it behind her back. Then, as she gazed into the grey eyes, laughing now at her so outrageously, her sense of humour got the better of her and she let out a chuckle.

"That's better. Now let's just run off a couple of letters, and I'll leave you in peace."

In peace, Margaret thought wistfully after he had gone. If he only knew!

In the weeks that followed, Margaret accepted two more invitations from William Pettigrew. He had also been to the flat one Sunday for afternoon tea, and Mrs. Grant had voted him "very nice".

Margaret wrinkled her nose. "Oh, Mother! Your most damning comment! If you say someone is nice, you usually mean innocuous and rather dull."

Mrs. Grant smiled. "Well, you must admit he's not exactly handsome, and *must* you encourage him to talk so much? After all, he can't possibly think either of us are interested in what they do to rats in research laboratories. Though they aren't my favourite animal, after some of his stories I began to feel quite sorry for the poor things."

Margaret went away to wash up the tea things, and the subject was not discussed again. She was sure, though, that her mother and sister had talked about her friendship with the doctor. When next she went to see Jean there had been a decidedly speculative look in her eye.

Easter fell at the end of March, and Margaret had arranged for her mother to go down to Bournemouth for one week before and one week after Easter week-end. With the cheque from Nicholas Hollis and in other ways she had managed to save the cost of a fortnight at the nursing home.

One morning early in March, Margaret was taking dictation from Mrs. Hollis, when Mrs. Macgennis came into the room. She spoke hurriedly, "Someone is on the telephone asking for Miss Grant. I think her mother has been taken ill. Shall I put the call through here?"

Before Margaret could answer, Mrs. Hollis said quickly, "Yes, by all means. Take the call here, Margaret."

Margaret walked quickly over and lifted the receiver. Almost at once she heard Mrs. Willis say, "Is that you, Miss Margaret? Your mother isn't well. Could you come home, please, right away?"

"Yes, of course. Have you called the doctor, Willie?"

"He's on his way," was the reply.

Margaret had been standing at the telephone with her back to the door, so she did not notice Nicholas walk into the room, nor see him raise his brows in inquiry. Mrs. Hollis was explaining the situation in a low voice when Margaret turned from the telephone.

"Mrs. Willis seems to think it may be serious. Would you mind if I caught the next train home, please?"

"No, you must go at once," Mrs. Hollis replied. "What time is the next train? Do you know?"

Before Margaret could reply, Nicholas broke in. "Never mind the trains. I'll take you down. The car is outside."

"No, I couldn't bother you." Margaret was beginning to collect her things hurriedly.

"Nonsense! I'll see you outside in three minutes."

They did not talk very much on the drive down to Bromley. Margaret spent most of the journey looking through the window and wondering how she would find her mother when she arrived home.

As they turned at last into the familiar road, they were just in time to see an ambulance draw away from the curb. The doctor was on the point of climbing into his own car as Nicholas drew up, and Margaret was out of the car and running towards the doctor's car, almost before he had stopped.

"Dr. James! Dr. James!"

The doctor, who had known her since she was a schoolgirl, turned and came back towards her.

"Ah, there you are, Margaret. I've arranged for your

mother to be admitted to hospital. The ambulance has just left."

"Yes, I saw it. Is she very ill?" Margaret asked.

"Well, she's had another stroke and I think she'll be better in hospital for a day or two. You'll be able to go and visit her."

"Another stroke!" Margaret's voice broke on the words. "But she's been so much better the last few months, and I've watched to see she doesn't overdo things, really I have."

"Now don't start blaming yourself," Dr. James reassured her. "There is simply no accounting for when these small haemorrhages will take place. Your mother will be all right, I assure you, but she's going to need careful nursing for a while, and that's why I thought she would be better in hospital. You could go there now if you wish. She'll be admitted to Ward B.3. Ask for Sister Steward and tell her I sent you."

"Thank you, I will. And thank you for coming so quickly."

With a brief handshake and a goodbye, the doctor got back into his car. Margaret suddenly recollected that she had jumped out of Nicholas's car without a thought or a word of thanks, and she turned now to where he was standing on the pavement, waiting for her to finish talking to the doctor.

"Thank you, Mr. Hollis. It was very good of you to bring me down here so quickly. I'm sorry I dashed off without thanking you just now, but I wanted to catch Dr. James."

"So I saw," Nicholas replied. "Now what? I take it that your mother has gone to hospital?"

"Yes. I'm going in to see Mrs. Willis and then I shall go round to the hospital and see how Mother is. Thank you once again for your kindness."

Nicholas gave a gesture of exasperation. "For heaven's sake, girl, stop the thank-yous! Let's get in and reassure your Mrs. Mop, then we can go and see how your mother is getting along."

Margaret looked uncomfortable. "But I don't like . . ."

Nicholas startled her by taking her arm and forcibly marching her up the garden path. "If ever there was an argumentative . . . By the Lord Harry! Do you or don't you want to get to the hospital as soon as you can?" Then he stopped suddenly as he saw the expression on Margaret's face. The scowl left his face and he looked down, his expression serious, almost pitying. "Sorry to bark at you, but come along, there's a good girl. Tell your Mrs. Willis what you want, and then let's get going."

Without another word, Margaret inserted her key and went into the flat. The sound of weeping from the direction of the kitchen made her realize that their wonderful Mrs. Willis was taking Mrs. Grant's collapse very much to heart. Margaret pushed the kitchen door open. "Don't cry, Willie dear. Mother will be all right, you'll see. The doctor says I can go and see her now, so stay here until I get back. Then I'll be able to tell you how she is."

Mrs. Willis mopped her eyes. She nodded, not trusting her voice.

Margaret turned and went out again. She shut the front door to see Nicholas leaning against the gate, smoking. He straightened up when he saw her coming, and held the gate open. He helped her into the passenger seat of the car and then climbed in himself.

He didn't start the car immediately, but got out his cigarette case and lighted another cigarette. When it was drawing, he handed it to Margaret without a word. She took it, looking at him in surprise.

"Do you good. Smoke it," and he started the car. "Tell me which way to go."

Margaret directed him to the local hospital. Nicholas drove straight into the car park and deftly inserted the car into the small space left between an opulent-looking Jaguar and a Mini. Margaret was opening her mouth to thank him once again, when he forestalled her.

"I'm coming in with you," he said.

Margaret didn't reply, merely opened her door and got out. When he had locked the car they walked over to the hospital entrance.

The ward sister was most kind and reassuring when Margaret and Nicholas were finally shown into her office, but she was firm in refusing to let Margaret see her mother. "She's been given a sedative and is resting nicely, Miss Grant. Come this evening at seven o'clock and if she's awake, she will be very glad to see you, I know. Now, can you bring some more things in for her at the same time? I've made a list here of what she'll need."

She handed Margaret a slip of paper, which she tucked into her handbag.

"Is it a very severe stroke, Sister?" she asked.

"Now, I'm not able to say until your mother has been under observation for a few days. Let me see, today's Wednesday. I should think by the week-end, we shall know. I'll ask the doctor to see you on Saturday."

Margaret thanked her and turned to Nicholas. He tucked her hand in his arm and led her out to the car. When they were settled in their seats once more and he had the engine running, he turned to her.

"I expect you want to let your sister know. Shall I take you over to her now?"

Margaret looked faintly surprised. She hadn't realized that Nicholas knew so much about her family.

"No, take me home, please. I'll phone my brother-in-law. Jean is having another baby and I think it would be better if Clive broke the news to her gently."

Nicholas nodded in agreement and reversed the car on to the road. They drove the short distance to the Grants' flat in silence. When Margaret was looking for her key, Nicholas said, "Keep Mother and me posted of what goes on, will you?"

Margaret had by this time found her key, and the door was standing open. "Yes, of course. Thank you once again, Mr. Hollis." Then in a diffident voice, "I suppose you wouldn't like a cup of coffee or something?"

"Many thanks, but no." He looked at his watch. "As a matter of fact I've a lunch appointment at one-thirty, so I'll be off," and with a brief salute he walked to his car.

Margaret went indoors, and after setting Mrs. Willis's mind at rest, she rang her brother-in-law at his office and told him the bad news.

"Jean and I will both come over to the hospital this evening," he said when he heard what the ward sister had suggested. "We'll meet you there."

Mrs. Willis left to go home after cooking a light lunch which neither she nor Margaret had the heart to enjoy. Margaret sat on afterwards smoking and drinking a second cup of coffee. When her cup was empty she fetched the list Sister Steward had given her and began to collect the things which her mother would require during her stay in hospital. As she folded nightdresses, a dressing gown and a spare bedjacket, she was suddenly reminded that she would have to cancel her mother's holiday. Easter was only a fortnight away, and it didn't seem very likely that Mrs. Grant would be fit to go even a short journey by then.

Margaret put the suitcase by the front door, tidied up the flat and then washed out a few undies to while away the time. She found that she could not sit still, and it was a real relief when the time came for her to leave for the hospital.

Jean and Clive were waiting outside when she arrived, and the three of them joined the queue of relatives waiting for the porter to open the doors. When they

101

were allowed in to see their mother, Margaret and Jean were permitted only a brief five minutes at her bedside. She obviously recognized them and gave a small smile before closing her eyes again. They sat on either side of the bed, holding her hands between their own, and afraid to meet each other's eyes. When Sister came quietly behind the screens and beckoned them to come out, they followed her into her office.

Jean was wiping her eyes with a small handkerchief.

Sister Steward looked at her as she sat down behind her desk. "Try not to worry. Your mother will look better when you come tomorrow, you know. Now, I've had a word with the doctor, and he is going to do some tests when Mrs. Grant is well enough. He should know the results by the week-end and I've arranged for you to see him on Saturday at three o'clock. Will that be all right?"

"Thank you, Sister. I can manage that." Margaret looked inquiringly at Jean.

"Yes," her sister said, "Clive can look after the twins while I come here with you, Margaret."

After they had taken her home, Clive and Jean came in for a quick cup of coffee. They arranged to meet at the hospital again the following evening, then left to allow their baby-sitter to go home.

The flat felt strangely empty to Margaret without her mother's happy presence. Though she had not had good health for many years, Mrs. Grant had never allowed her disability to affect her temper, and it was always a sunny smile and a pleasant greeting which met Margaret each evening.

When she got to bed that night, Margaret was unable to sleep. What is going to happen, she mused, if Mother is going to be a hopeless invalid after this? I can't nurse her and go out to work, and Jean certainly can't have her to live with them if there's another baby on the way. Midnight saw her still staring into the darkness. Sleep was far away, so she got up and made some tea. Sitting at the kitchen table, sipping it, she hardly dared to think about the future.

Mrs. Hollis was most surprised when Margaret arrived for work at the usual time next morning.

"There was no point in my staying at home, Mrs. Hollis," Margaret explained. "I rang the hospital first thing this morning, and Mother is about the same. I've given them this telephone number in case they want me urgently. I hope you don't mind."

"Of course not. But I feel you shouldn't have come in at all, my dear," was the reply.

"I can't sit still at home. Really, I prefer to work," Margaret said. "It takes my mind off things."

Mrs. Hollis gave an understanding smile, and they got on with the day's work. A little later, as she was going down to the office, Margaret met Nicholas.

After he had wished her good morning he said, "How is your mother?"

Margaret told him what the ward sister had said and he nodded and went on his way.

When Jean and Margaret arrived at the hospital the following Saturday, they were taken at once to see the doctor who was in charge of their mother's ward. He was a kindly, grey-haired physician, who immediately put the girls at their ease.

He opened a file on the desk, and leaning his elbows on it, smiled across at them.

"Now, take off those solemn expressions. Your mother isn't going to die, you know. Not this time, at any rate." He turned over two or three papers before continuing. "However, from now on you've got to face up to the fact that she has complete paralysis of her left arm and leg. She may regain a little movement after she's had physiotherapy, but she'll always be handicapped."

Margaret and her sister looked at each other, aghast.

"Now, is there anything you'd like to ask me?"

Margaret found her voice. "Yes, Doctor. Can you tell us how long Mother will be in hospital, and whether you think she will ever be able to lead a moderately normal life again?"

"Well, she will have to be in hospital for two or three weeks at least. In about ten days or so we shall start exercises, and then see how she does. As to leading a normal life—I'm afraid you must face the fact that your mother has now had two cerebral haemorrhages. You are very fortunate in that she is still alive. With care, she may live a great many more years, but she will never be able to walk properly again or without the help of crutches or a stick."

He looked inquiringly at the two girls. "I take it that you are both prepared to do all you can to help your mother rehabilitate herself, as, I understand from Dr. James, you did after her first stroke?"

Tears were beginning to run slowly down Jean's cheeks, so Margaret answered for both of them. "Of course, Doctor. We shall do all we can. Thank you for seeing us. May we go up and see Mother now?"

The doctor nodded and rose to his feet. "If you want to see me at any time, just ask the ward sister to arrange it, will you?" and he opened the door and pointed out the nearest way to reach their mother's ward.

Jean held Margaret's arm tightly as they went upstairs. By the time they had reached the first floor, she had dried her eyes and composed herself. "Mustn't let Mother guess I'm upset," she whispered to Margaret as they approached the bedside.

Mrs. Grant was patently pleased to see her daughters come into the ward. She moved her right hand and smiled as they kissed her. "Have you seen my roses?" she asked.

Jean and Margaret both turned to look at the bedside locker. On it was a vase containing over a dozen magnificent flame-coloured roses. There was a card at the foot of the vase and Jean bent down and read aloud, "With kindest regards, Alicia, Nicholas and Miles Hollis. My goodness, Mother, they're gorgeous! They must think you're Elizabeth Taylor, at least."

Mrs. Grant smiled at this. "Sit down, both of you. Let me look at you. Stupid of me to be ill like this."

Margaret and Jean found chairs and sat down on either side of the bed. The three of them talked quiety until it was time for visitors to leave, then they kissed their mother and with a "See you tomorrow, darling", the sisters walked slowly down to the car. They both sat for several moments without speaking. Then as Jean put her finger on the starter she said, "Awful to see Mother like that again, isn't it? I thought she'd quite got over that first stroke, and now for this to happen. It never occurred to me that she might have another. What are we going to do, Margaret, if she doesn't get any better? She won't be able to stay in hospital for very long—you know how short of beds they always are."

"Yes, I know," Margaret replied. "Well, let's cross that bridge when we come to it. At the moment, we can only hope she'll do better than the doctor thinks. I'd back Mother any time. She's so resilient. Remember last time we never thought she'd ever get better, but she was determined to get on her feet again and she did."

"Umm, yes, but I think this time it's much more serious," Jean answered.

Margaret secretly agreed with her, but thought there was no point in saying so. It wouldn't do her sister any good to have a lot of worry just now, and to take Jean's mind off the problem she started to ask after the twins, whom she had not seen for several days.

All the next week, Margaret worked hard, staying later in the evenings now there was no occasion to hurry home. After a hasty snack, she usually went straight to the hospital to see her mother.

Mrs. Hollis had told her that she must take any time off she wished, but since visiting was in the evenings during week-days, that had not been necessary. Margarét had thanked her for the flowers, and as she did so had surprised a smile on Mrs. Hollis's face, which on anyone else would have been called a grin.

"I'm glad your mother liked them, my dear," Mrs. Hollis said, the mischievous smile still lighting the grey eyes so like her elder son's. "Nicholas chose them." Then without further comment on the subject of the roses, she picked up a letter and began to dictate a reply.

As Margaret's pencil flew over the notebook, she was still wondering what had caused the amusement she had seen in Mrs. Hollis's face. Surely she could not be thinking . . . No, that was impossible. Margaret was positive that her employer could have no idea of her innermost feelings towards Nicholas. Something else must have caused that impish smile—something to do with the roses, since they had been talking about them at the time.

CHAPTER SEVEN

IT was with mixed feelings of surprise and yet resignation, therefore, that the following Saturday afternoon Margaret walked into the ward to find Nicholas Hollis already sitting at her mother's bedside. He rose when he saw her, and fetched another chair.

"Hello, dear! Jean not coming this afternoon?" Mrs. Grant asked as Margaret bent and kissed her cheek. As she sat down, trying in vain not to meet the amused glance from the other side of the bed she replied, "No. The twins are going to a birthday party, so I suggested to Jean that she came to see you tomorrow instead. I knew you'd understand."

"Of course," Mrs. Grant said. "And in any case, I've had a lovely surprise today with Nicholas dropping in. Look what he's brought me."

She turned to the bedside locker, and Margaret then noticed the attractive basket of fruit which stood upon it.

"You'll be popular with the nurses," Margaret laughed, "for they'll know you could never eat so much fruit on your own."

Nicholas joined in the general laugh. "That was the idea. I know how glamorous nurses are these days, and I want to get well in with them."

He glanced round the ward, where two probationers were busy carrying out their afternoon duties. "Which one do you suggest I cultivate, Mrs. Grant? The blonde or that dark one with the curls?"

Mrs. Grant joined in the game with almost her usual twinkle lighting her eyes. "Oh, the dark one, definitely. She's always talking about how she's going to travel when she finishes her training, or even be a missionary."

Nicholas rubbed his hands together. "The very one! She can start by converting me."

Heads turned as Mrs. Grant and Margaret both broke into fits of laughter. Nicholas was looking unashamedly at the dark nurse as she hurried down the ward in his direction, and was ostentatiously straightening his tie and smoothing down his unruly, short hair. Though she could not have heard what they had been saying, the nurse could see that everyone within earshot of Mrs. Grant's bed was looking at her. Nicholas's gestures were unmistakable and she blushed a becoming pink as she went past.

"Poor child!" Mrs. Grant said. "I shall have to explain that some of my friends are mad, but quite harmless."

Nicholas laughed with her. He rose to his feet and took her hand. "It's been lovely seeing you for a few minutes, Mrs. Grant. I'll leave your daughter to entertain you now. Get well soon, won't you? I'll look in again one day," and with a brief wave to Margaret, he was gone.

As the ward doors shut to behind him, there was a few moments' silence.

"I was very surprised to see him," Mrs. Grant said. "Did you know he was coming?"

"No." Margaret pretended to be sorting the letters she had brought with her. "Though it was very kind of him, wasn't it?" She gave her mother no opportunity to question her further by saying, "Now here are your letters. Most of them came this morning. Do you want me to read them to you? There's one from Aunt Mary. I wrote last week-end to tell her you were in hospital."

Margaret did not tell her mother that she had herself received a separate letter from Mary Salmon, urging Margaret to send Mrs. Grant down for her convalescence to Bournemouth. She could see how slow this time her mother was in responding to treatment, and Margaret was rather dreading her next interview with the doctor, and hearing what he would have to say.

Though she was unaware of this, the constant strain and anxiety of her mother's illness were beginning to show in her face. There was dark shadows under Margaret's eyes and she had lost her usual delicate colour.

When she was straightening her office the following Friday evening, and beginning to get ready to go for her train, Nicholas Hollis strolled into the room.

"Did you want some letters done?" Margaret asked quickly.

"No. I came to see if you were ready to leave. I'll take you for some food and then run you to the hospital. I take it you are going to see your mother this evening?"

"Yes. But I've got to go home first for some things I've left ready to take with me."

"Well, all right. We'll stop at a delicatessen and buy something for a quick supper."

Margaret stopped what she was doing in sheer astonishment. What a surprising man he was! She glanced at him and saw he was prepared to argue with her about it. Bending her head to hide a smile, she said, "Well, fine! I'll just get my coat, then I'm ready."

"What? No argument? No 'please don't trouble yourself, Mr. Hollis' "—he mimicked her in precise tones.

Margaret smiled. "No, no arguments. Surprised?"

"Very," Nicholas replied as he held the door open for her.

When Margaret came out of the cloakroom, he was waiting in the hall, his overcoat already on and a hat in his hand. He took her elbow as he walked her out to the car. When he had seen her comfortably seated he went round and slipped into his own seat.

It was raining steadily as they came to a brief halt at the first set of traffic lights. Margaret was very relieved to be going home in a comfortable car, instead of having to face the usual crush in the train. This evening there would have been the added discomfort of everyone wearing mackintoshes and carrying dripping umbrellas.

Nicholas pulled up before a lighted shop and with a hasty "stop there" got out and ran across the wet pavement. He came out a few minutes later with a couple of tins in his hands, a wrapped parcel and a long loaf of French bread tucked under his arm.

He climbed back into the car and tossed them on to the rear seat, then he started the car again and they drove out to Bromley, picking their way through the busy homebound traffic.

Margaret had her key ready as the car drew up at the

flat, and they were soon inside. It felt cold and she said diffidently, "The only warm spot will be the kitchen. Do you mind?"

"Why on earth should I? Lead on."

Margaret opened the kitchen door, and sure enough the stove glowed warmly. She walked over and opened the damper, raking the smouldering fuel into a bright flame.

"I don't know what I'd do without Mrs. Willis. She comes in and makes it up during the afternoon, though I've told her several times not to bother."

While she had been dealing with the stove, Nicholas had been searching the cupboards. He had found a plate and was unwrapping the parcel. It contained a succulent roast chicken. "Where's the carving knife and your tin-opener?" he asked, and throwing his overcoat on to a chair he walked to the kitchen sink and commenced to wash his hands.

Margaret took off her own coat and then started to lay the table. One of the tins she discovered contained potato salad, and the other asparagus. She soon had them open and had turned the contents on to two dishes. Butter, a fresh slab of crumbly Cheshire cheese, and the loaf of French bread were put out, and then, as Nicholas started to carve the chicken, Margaret filled the coffee percolator and switched it on.

They sat down and started to eat, almost in silence. When they had emptied their plates, Margaret filled two cups with coffee, and placed one at Nicholas's right hand. He sat back and sighed with satisfaction.

"Now that was a really satisfying snack, wasn't it?" He cut a huge wedge of cheese as he spoke and transferred it to his side plate.

Margaret gaped with astonishment. When she saw him start to grin she hastily closed her mouth.

"I was just going to remark too on the way we fell to on the food simultaneously without any need for words.

Might be an old married couple, mightn't we, Meg?"

He watched delightedly as the colour rose in a great wave to her face.

"You never fail, dear girl. It's sheer bliss to find a girl who can blush these days. Usually it's me they put to the blush. The majority seem to have usurped all our masculine attributes. Our trousers, our wage packets, and most modern girls even swear like men these days. I've not met a girl like you for years. I was beginning to think they were all extinct."

Margaret's colour subsided slowly. "You've been moving in the wrong circles, then. Nearly all my friends are exactly like me and have the same standards."

"Um, well, you may be right." He glanced at his watch. "Just time for a cigarette, and then if we're to get to the hospital by seven, I think we'd better go, don't you?"

They sat on smoking their cigarettes and when they had finished their coffee, drove to the hospital. In the car park, they were just in time to see Jean and Clive drive up and park. Margaret introduced the two men, and while she and her sister went up to see Mrs. Grant, Clive and Nicholas sat down to wait in the hospital out-patient department.

When Margaret and Jean came out an hour later, however, Nicholas had gone. Clive sauntered up to them as he saw them emerge with the rest of the evening visitors, and said, "Hollis had to go, Margaret. I said we'd take you home."

"Except when he smiles, he's a cynical-looking individual, I must say," said Jean. "How did he come to be driving you here tonight, Margaret?"

Though she explained the circumstances, Margaret omitted to tell her sister that they had first stopped at the flat for an intimate meal together.

During the weeks that followed, Mrs. Grant's progress was slow. When she had been in hospital for about

111

five weeks, Margaret received a phone call from William Pettigrew.

"I've just come back from a conference in Denmark," he announced as soon as they had exchanged preliminary remarks. "Miles tells me that you've sickness in the family. Your mother, isn't it?"

Margaret explained what had happened.

"Sorry to hear it, old girl. Won't stop you having a spot of dinner with me one evening, though, will it?"

"No," Margaret replied slowly, "but it would have to be at the week-end. Will that be all right?"

"Certainly. Shall we say Saturday, then? I'll meet you in at the station if you let me know which train you'll be coming on."

Arrangements were made for them to meet the following Saturday. When Margaret and Jean arrived for afternoon visiting on that day, however, they were stopped by Sister Steward as they were going into the ward.

"Can you spare me a few minutes after visiting?" she asked as they paused in her office doorway.

"I wonder what she wants?" Jean said quietly, as she and Margaret made their way towards Mrs. Grant's bed.

Sister Steward was sitting behind her desk when they knocked on her door at the close of visiting hours. She gave them both a chair, and they sat down facing her.

"Now I want to see you about your mother's discharge," she began. "Doctor feels we can't help her any more here, and he suggests you get her into a good convalescent home for a month or two. The almoner would help you about that if you don't know one."

"Is Mother going to get any better than she is now?" Jean inquired.

"Well," Sister looked quietly across the desk at the two sisters, "you must face the fact that this is the second stroke your mother has had. She isn't young and you mustn't expect miracles. She has got her speech

112

back perfectly and some slight movement in the left hand, which I must admit when she was first brought in I never thought possible. I'm afraid, though, she's unlikely to ever get more than the partial return of full movement to her left leg, and I doubt if she'll ever walk again without some assistance."

Margaret saw the tears rising to her sister's eyes. She stood up. "Thank you very much, Sister, for telling us. Shall I go and see the almoner now?"

Sister glanced at her watch. "I'm afraid she wouldn't be in now, but if you come early on Monday evening, I will arrange for you to see her then. Will that do?"

Margaret thanked her and the two girls left the hospital almost in silence. When they were outside and seated in Jean's car, they got out cigarettes and lit up. They smoked in silence for a moment or two.

"What are we going to do? Afterwards, I mean," Jean said. "Mother won't be able to stay in a convalescent home for ever, and you can't look after a helpless invalid and go out to work at the same time. I'm out of the running with this baby on the way. And, in any case, where is the money to come from to pay for the home?"

Margaret tipped ash off her cigarette before she answered. "There's Mother's annuity. With what I can add and perhaps a little you and Clive would contribute, perhaps we'll be able to manage."

"Oh, Margaret, be your age! You're living in cloud cuckoo land. The convalescent home, or any nursing home for that matter, will cost in the teens of guineas. Look what Aunt Mary has to pay."

Margaret sighed. "Yes, I know. If only we had a bit of capital! Aunt Mary's nursing home would be the answer, of course. Mother wouldn't fret down there with her. Anyway, Jean, it's no good worrying yet. Wait until I've heard what the almoner has to say on Monday. Maybe she can come up with an answer."

Jean leaned forward and started the car. "Yes, and I can guess what she'll say when you tell her what we can afford. Remember that place poor Mrs. Rigby was taken to?"

She was referring to an old friend of the family's who had been taken ill three or four years before. Without relatives, she had been relegated eventually to an old people's home run by an untidy-looking ex-nurse and her husband. Mrs. Grant and daughters had driven down to see her on one never-to-be-forgotten day shortly before the old lady had died.

It was a quiet, pensive companion that William Pettigrew took out that evening. However, as he was busy most of the evening telling Margaret about the conference he had just attended, her silence went unnoticed.

"Go to see your mother every day, do you?" he asked before he left her that evening. "Well, in that case, I'll drive you down on Monday. What time?"

Margaret told him, and let herself into the flat, relieved to be alone at last to think.

On Monday afternoon, Nicholas strolled into her office.

"It's raining again," he announced. "I'll run you down to the hospital this evening."

Margaret looked up from her work. "Thanks, but I've had the offer of a lift." She smiled as she spoke.

Nicholas didn't answer for a moment, but stood contemplating her, a moody look on his face.

"Your brother-in-law?"

Margaret looked down at her hands. "No. A friend." She didn't know why she didn't say who it was. After all, Nicholas knew William Pettigrew well.

"I see. Well, so long as you aren't going to get a wetting," and he strolled out as if he had done his duty and was relieved that his services had not been required after all.

However, as Margaret was leaving the house, she

found him on the steps, obviously just on the point of going out, and talking to Dr. Pettigrew, who had just arrived to collect her.

"Ah, there you are, my dear. Jump in before you get wet."

As William handed her into the car, Margaret couldn't resist a glance at Nicholas. He was coming down the steps, his brows raised in a very quizzical manner.

"Bother," thought Margaret. Now why had he to be going out at just this moment?"

When she saw the almoner, Margaret was anything but reassured. Mrs. Grant, she was told, could go for a fortnight to a Health Service convalescent home, free of charge. After that, if she still required trained nursing, she would have to be moved to a private home. The almoner gave Margaret a list of nursing and convalescent homes, and suggested she write asking their terms and whether in fact they had a vacancy.

During a few free moments the following day, Margaret sat down and wrote to all the homes on the list. She also called at two nursing homes in the immediate vicinity of her home. Both were obviously under excellent management, but in each case the charges were high.

When the replies to her letters arrived, these too were not encouraging. Out of the ten addresses to which Margaret had written, six replied to say that they had no vacancies for at least six months, three quoted charges far in excess of what the Grants could afford, and the last one offered a vacancy in one month's time. Though the charges quoted were modest, something about the wording of the reply left Margaret feeling uneasy.

When she went over to visit her sister that night, Margaret took the replies with her. Clive and the two girls read them through together.

Clive was the first to speak. "Nothing here seems much

good. How about us going down to look at this place, though." He tapped the letter which had promised a vacancy in a month's time. Margaret looked across at her sister and brother-in-law. "I was wondering . . ." she began, "if I gave up the flat and sold the furniture, would you two have me here?"

"But . . ." Jean began. Clive interrupted her. "If it would help, Margaret, you know we'd gladly have you here. But would it? The furniture wouldn't bring in much at today's prices. Even with that, your mother's annuity and what we three could contribute, we still couldn't pay twenty-five or thirty guineas a week, which is what these people are asking." He tapped the letters on the table.

"Then the only other solution is for me to leave Mrs. Hollis and nurse Mother myself," said Margaret. "Perhaps I could get copy-typing to do at home. That would help."

Jean got up and walked round the table to her sister. "No good, dear. Even then you just couldn't manage. Now could you? Let's face facts."

Margaret brushed the hair off her forehead wearily. "No, I suppose you're right. I'll go down on Sunday and see this place, if you two will visit Mother. Don't tell her where I've gone, though. I'll think of some excuse for not going in to see her."

Twice during that week, Nicholas offered her a lift to the hospital, but on each occasion Margaret found some excuse for refusing. With the problem of her mother's future on her mind, she had decided that she would try and see no more of Nicholas than she could help. The intimate meal they had shared in the flat had opened her eyes to the fact that she had become far too interested in her employer's disturbing elder son. She knew now that what she had termed "infatuation" was rapidly sliding into wholehearted love. He was only being kind, she decided, probably at his mother's instigation, in offering help during Mrs. Grant's stay in hospital, and for her own peace of mind it would be wiser to refuse his assistance.

As she travelled down to the outer London district to look over the nursing home the following Sunday, her thoughts strayed to day-dreaming. "If only" figured largely in her mind. If only she had been beautiful, madly attractive or even amongst Nicholas Hollis's circle of intimate friends. Margaret took herself to task. It was futile to think along these lines. In any case, Nicholas seemed to have his pick of many beautiful girls, as far as she could judge from comments Mrs. Macgennis let fall and the number of times the telephone rang for him. And so far he didn't appear to have singled one out for special attention.

From the outside, the nursing home looked worse than Margaret had feared when she had seen how modest was the weekly charge. The house itself looked gloomy, sadly in need of repair and a coat of paint. The door was opened to her ring by an elderly maid who was extremely deaf. It took Margaret three minutes or more to make her understand that she wanted to see the person in charge.

Margaret waited ten minutes in an untidy room before the matron of the nursing home appeared. Though she wore a clean white uniform, Margaret noticed her shoes needed cleaning and that a long trailing piece of untidy hair hung down under her nurse's cap.

Even more unimpressive was the home itself. As Margaret was taken round she saw that a general air of dilapidation hung about it, as if the person in charge did so much and then lost heart at really making everything shine and sparkle. Most of the patients too, Margaret noticed, were a good deal older than her mother. Those who could get up were sitting round a sitting-room overlooking the garden, looking as if they had been put there at breakfast time and were not expected to move until bedtime. They all looked up in such an apathetic way when she went in and murmured a shy

117

"good afternoon" that Margaret's heart sank. Though this place would have been within their means, she felt it would be a great mistake to bring here mother to live here.

Monday morning dawned cold, and when Margaret was getting ready to go to the station, it started to hail. By the time she was half-way there, the hail had turned to rain, and a steady downpour was descending pitilessly. She arrived at Mrs. Hollis's cold, wet, and feeling more depressed than ever.

It didn't improve matters when she recalled that there was a committee meeting that afternoon, at which both Blanche Miln-Prescott and her mother would doubtless be present. As she had feared, they came in just as Mrs. Hollis was opening the meeting. Margaret was aware once or twice when she was taking down the minutes that Blanche was glancing in her direction and then turning to whisper in her neighbour's ear. When the items on the agenda had all been discussed, Margaret overheard Blanche saying, in tones obviously intended to reach as many ears as possible, that "she wondered if dear Mrs. Hollis knew what was going on."

The week's events, coupled with the weather, had made Margaret feel as if her sensibilities had been numbed, and this obvious piece of malice, of which she could make no sense, left her unmoved. She went back to her office, but instead of getting on with typing out the minutes of the meeting, she started to make calculations on the back of a piece of paper. After twenty minutes of trying first one and then another combination of figures, it was obvious that the Grant finances were not going to work out to Margaret's satisfaction.

She stared at the paper, the tears gathering in her eyes. Why, oh, why, she asked herself, did Mother play ducks and drakes with Father's money? Now, if at no other time, they could have done with the capital he had left at his death.

Margaret was searching in her handbag for a handkerchief, when she heard steps rapidly approaching the office door. As it opened, she quickly turned her back, hastily wiping her eyes.

The door slammed to, but Margaret stood pretending to look into the darkened garden, knowing instinctively who had entered.

She was giving her eyes a last hasty rub when hands descended on her shoulders, and she was spun round to face the light. Nicholas Hollis's hard, grey eyes went over her tear-stained face deliberately. Then he removed his hands from her shoulders, and took out his cigarette case.

He took out two cigarettes and lighted them both, handing one to Margaret when it was drawing properly. Then he took a turn around the room, coming back to stand in front of her where she stood by the window, puffing nervously at the cigarette.

"Well?" he demanded. "Out with it. Something to do with your mother, is it?"

"In a way." Margaret moved away to sit at her desk, stubbing out the cigarette as she did so. "We're having trouble getting her into a suitable nursing home. It was stupid of me to cry about it." She looked up as she finished speaking and made a gallant attempt at a smile.

Nicholas pulled out a chair, and straddling it backwards, he rested his elbows along the back and gazed at her in silence for several moments.

"What about that place in Bournemouth?"

Margaret stirred restlessly. "Too expensive!"

She got up and nervously started to put some letters into their envelopes.

Nicholas didn't speak again for a minute.

"She'd be happy there, though, wouldn't she? Isn't there an old friend of your mother's living there already?"

"Yes," Margaret said shortly, "but it's out of the question."

Nicholas looked at her speculatively for a few moments before he again spoke. "I suppose you wouldn't be prepared to enter into a bargain to ensure your mother's welfare and happiness?"

Margaret put down an envelope and looked at him, a question in her eyes. "Bargain? What sort of bargain?"

Nicholas took his time before replying. Then he said, "A bargain between you and me. You marry me and in return I take care of your mother."

Margaret was speechless. Finally she said, "Is this a joke? You can't be serious."

Nicholas got to his feet. "It's not a joke, and I was never more serious in my life." He walked down the room and back again, until he was once more standing directly in front of Margaret. "It's a perfectly simple arrangement. You marry me before I return to Rhodesia, and I'll take over all your mother's financial and other commitments. I will, moreover, arrange for you to fly home regularly to visit her. What do you say?"

Margaret didn't say anything for a moment, but continued to search his face for a hint of his usual mockery. His expression was quite serious, however, and he was obviously waiting patiently for a reply.

"I still can't believe you're serious. Why should you want to help us in this way, let alone marry me? It doesn't make sense."

Nicholas never moved, but a smile lit his eyes.

"It makes sense to me. I want to get married. You want money to provide for your mother. What could be more sensible than that we get together? Now what do you say, Meg?"

It was the use of the dimunitive that stopped Margaret saying an immediate and decisive "no". She had a sudden swift recollection of their hour spent together that evening when she had gone down to help him with that second report. She stood there turning matters over in her mind. It still didn't make sense to her why

Nicholas should be suggesting such a bargain, but it would have two advantages where she was concerned. One was that her mother would receive every care and comfort if she accepted, and the other—yes, wasn't the other that if she accepted she would be getting her heart's desire? Hadn't she been deeply in love with Nicholas Hollis for some time now? It had come about despite her better judgement, despite the fact that she knew she was one of a long line of women all too ready to accept his attentions.

Before she could stop, a rash impulse overcame her saner self and she said quickly, "Yes, all right. If you'll see that Mother goes into the nursing home with Mrs. Salmon and has every comfort that money can buy, then I'll marry you."

It wasn't the most tactful of replies, and Margaret did not know what Nicholas would say in reply, but all he did was to smile slowly and say, "Good—that's settled. Do we seal it with a kiss?" Then, as Margaret looked at him uncertainly, "Never mind. I'll go and break the news to Mother and then I'll run you home. Wait for me," and he walked swiftly out of the room.

Margaret resumed putting up the post with hands that trembled. Somehow she still couldn't believe that she hadn't dreamed the whole preceding conversation.

By the time the office was cleared, and she had washed and put on her outdoor things, she was quite sure she had suffered from an hallucination. Nicholas had not returned, but when she went into the hall he was running down the stairs. He looked very pleased with himself and his words surprised her yet again.

"Can you wait a moment while I see Cook?"

Margaret nodded as he stepped through the door leading to the kitchen. Whatever could he want to see Cook about? He reappeared as quickly as he had gone and said, "Mother wants us to come upstairs to receive her blessing before we go, Meg. Have we time?"

Margaret looked nervously at her wristwatch. "Yes, I think so," she stammered as she walked up the stairs beside him.

She saw Nicholas glancing at her as they reached the upper floor. "Not nervous, are you?"

Margaret straightened her shoulders. Her chin lifted. "No, no, I'm not frightened."

He took her arm as he opened his mother's sitting-room door and said, almost under his breath, "That's my girl!"

Before she realized what he had said, Margaret was inside the room, and both Mrs. Hollis and Miles were rising to greet her. Mrs. Hollis came forward, her hands outstretched.

"My dear child! I couldn't be more delighted," and she kissed Margaret on both cheeks.

Still holding her hands, she said, "But what a surprise. Aren't they dark horses, Miles?" and she laughed over her shoulder.

Miles walked forward slowly. "Yes, it's a surprise. But a very pleasant one. My very best wishes to you both. Am I allowed to kiss my future sister-in-law?" he asked over Margaret's head.

She heard Nicholas laugh behind her. "By all means!" And Miles stooped his lanky frame and kissed her shyly on the cheek.

As he turned away he said, "This warrants a drink. What do you say, Mother?"

"Certainly, if Margaret has time before she goes to the hospital. Ring the bell, will you, Miles?"

"Quite unnecessary, Mum," Nicholas interrupted. "I've already ordered champagne, and here it comes, I think."

As he spoke, a knock fell on the door and Cook herself entered wearing an immaculate white apron, a tray of glasses and a tall bottle in her hands.

"Just at the right moment," Nicholas remarked.

"Fetch Nannie, will you, Cook, and we'll all have a toast to celebrate my engagement."

Cook's round face creased into a grin. "Very well, Mr. Nicholas, I'll fetch her at once." Then she turned to Margaret and said, "My best wishes, Miss Grant," before going away to fetch Mrs. Macgennis.

By the time she returned, a bewildered Mrs. Macgennis in tow, Nicholas had opened the champagne and the glasses had been filled. "Ah, there you are, Mac. Come and drink a toast. I've been hog-tied at last. Are you pleased?"

"Whatever do you mean, Master Nicky?"

Mrs. Hollis answered for him. "Nicholas and Margaret here are going to be married. Isn't it wonderful news, Nannie? We'd given up hoping, hadn't we?"

Mrs. Macgennis came over and took Margaret's hands in hers. The tears were streaming down her face. "Oh, Miss Grant dear, 'tis wonderful news indeed!" And under cover of the general conversation she whispered, "You will be good to my laddie, won't you?"

Margaret nodded as a glass was thrust into her hand. Nicholas gave one to Mrs. Macgennis and said, "Heavens, Mac, you haven't turned on the waterworks just because I've got engaged, have you? If so, heaven help us on the wedding day. You'll flood us out of church!"

In the general laughter, Margaret's feeling of nervousness vanished completely. She was quiet in the car driving down to the hospital. Events were happening so quickly she felt breathless.

Nicholas too had been silent during the first part of the journey. As he stopped at a red light, he glanced sideways at her.

"Not regretting your decision, are you?" he asked.

"No, but things are happening a bit too quickly. I'm beginning to think I'm having a dream."

"Sure you don't mean a nightmare?" he gibed gently. Margaret did not reply, so he went on. "I think I'd better put an announcement in the papers before you can change your mind," he murmured outrageously. "You'll have to tell me your father's christian name, though, and your mother's too. I don't think I've ever heard you mention it."

"It's Paula," Margaret said quietly.

"Very nice, I like that," Nicholas said. Then he laughed, "Perhaps she'd like us to call the first girl after her."

His eyes were full of mockery as he spoke. Margaret blushed in the dusk of the car. When she'd promised an hour ago to marry Nicholas, she hadn't thought about a future family. Now as she contemplated to what she was committed, her heart beat faster.

As the lights changed, Nicholas spoke again. "Will your sister be at the hospital this evening?"

"No, Jean won't be going tonight."

"Good, then we can both go in and break the news to your mother."

Margaret said quickly, "I think it would be better if I told Mother and Jean about our engagement. Without you there, I mean." She stopped suddenly, aware that she was expressing herself badly. "What I mean is . . . She stopped as the car drew up before her own front gate.

Nicholas turned sideways and put on the inside light. He contemplated her flushed and confused face for a moment or two. "Let's get one thing quite straight, Meg. There's going to be no suspicion of a hole-and-corner affair about this engagement. I shall see your mother and sister tonight, and together we shall tell them we intend getting married in about three months' time. Then tomorrow I shall arrange about getting you an engagement ring. Now is that quite clearly understood?"

Margaret was surprised at the firm, forthright tones. "Yes. But surely there's no need to get a ring? I'd far rather . . ."

Nicholas held up his hand. "We can discuss this better over a meal. Let's get inside. It's cold out here. I've brought some eats from home. Cook rifled the fridge while we were getting ready."

Margaret opened the passenger door and got out in silence. There seemed no point in arguing; she was obviously going to be overruled. They walked up to the front door and Nicholas took the key out of her hand.

In silence they switched on the lights and went into the kitchen. Nicholas put a couple of packages on to the table, and without a word, went to the stove and stirred in into a brighter blaze. Margaret took off her coat and ran a hand through her hair.

Nicholas looked over his shoulder and grinned. "Still looking a bit bewildered, beloved? Food is what you need. Open the parcels, will you?"

Margaret went away to hang up her outdoor things, and then came back and started to prepare the supper. As she arranged chops, sausages, kidneys and tomatoes in the griller she said, "Isn't it a bit early for you to have a meal?"

"Good heavens, girl, I can eat any time. Now where are the plates?"

As they were sitting down to the meal, Nicholas suddenly said, "It won't be necessary to tell your mother about the financial arrangements, will it?"

Margaret cut a sausage in half before replying.

"No, she's quite hopeless really over money. I don't think the cost of the nursing home will register with her. She'll just accept anything Jean and I arrange for her. But my sister will have to be told. You know, don't you, that Mother was left fairly well off when Father died? She took some bad advice, realized all his safe investments and was persuaded to risk the capital."

Margaret looked down at her plate, unwilling to have to confide in him her mother's past mistakes. When she glanced up again, it was into his intent eyes. "I don't have to tell you that the gamble didn't pay off. My sister's father-in-law did what he could, but he didn't salvage a quarter of it."

Nicholas continued eating for a few minutes before replying.

"I see. I must admit I've wondered once or twice why you and your mother seemed to be so hard up. Your mother's reminiscences, while we were down in Kent, all gave me the picture of a much more comfortable life."

Margaret's smile was wistful. "Yes, we had a pretty wonderful time when Father was alive. We had a lovely home, Jean and I went to boarding school, and I was about to go abroad for a year to polish up my languages when he died. We did manage to keep Jean at school until she was seventeen, but I had to leave and get a job."

Nicholas, she found, was watching her as she made this explanation. The expression in the grey eyes unnerved her, and Margaret hastily put down her knife and fork, and got up to fuss unnecessarily with the coffee percolator.

Mrs. Grant took the news of Margaret's engagement with the merest chuckle. She pulled her daughter to her without comment, kissed her, then turned to Nicholas. Her eyes twinkled as she took his hand. "I won't congratulate you, Nicholas, that would seem like patting myself on the back, but I will say how pleased I am with Margaret's choice. When I'm gone, I know now that both my girls will be in good hands."

"Now, Mother," Margaret interrupted her, "this is a happy occasion. Let's have no remarks like that. You're going to dance at my wedding and later come and visit Nicholas and me. You wait and see!"

Mrs. Grant released Nicholas's hand and smiled, but she did not reply. When she spoke a moment or so later it was on quite a different subject, and she did not refer to the engagement again until they were leaving at the

126

end of the visiting hour. As Margaret kissed her good-bye, she whispered in her ear, "I'm so glad, darling. I know you love him."

As they walked back to the car, Margaret hoped Nicholas would think her high colour was due to the warmth of the hospital heating.

Jean and Clive, if they felt any surprise, successfully hid it. Jean kissed her sister warmly, then, on the pretext of needing help with supper, carried Margaret off to the kitchen.

As soon as the door was closed she turned. "Now then, out with it! You could have knocked me down with a feather when you walked in and dropped your bombshell. I didn't know he'd even taken you out."

Margaret laughed to cover her nervousness. "He hasn't—well apart from giving me lifts from time to time. The fact is, Jean, Nicholas found me in tears this evening. Utterly stupid of me, wasn't it, but I was so worried about Mother, and I'd had quite a day too. I suppose the miseries just got the better of me. Well, anyway, he proposed on the understanding that if I married him, he'd take over all Mother's expenses. I find I do like him very much, so I said 'yes'." Margaret smiled as she turned to her sister.

"Don't look so worried. I'm quite happy about it. After all, I'm twenty-seven on my next birthday and I don't suppose I'll ever get a better offer."

Jean looked at her sister for a few moments in silence before she turned away and started to fill the kettle. She lighted the gas under it before she spoke.

"I must admit, if he intends to cope with Mother's finances it will be a tremendous load off our minds. But are you really sure you want to marry him? Not long ago you were breathing fire and smoke every time his name was mentioned."

"Yes, I do want to marry him, Jean. Let's leave it at that, shall we?"

Jean smiled and nodded. "Just so long as you aren't

offering yourself as a sacrifice on the maternal altar. Marriage to the right person can be such fun, but I imagine it could be as much hell with the wrong one."

When the sisters wheeled in a light supper tray on the trolley, they found the two men deep in conversation. It was obvious that Clive and Nicholas had taken to each other, and Jean had to speak twice before they could be persuaded to terminate what was obviously, to them, a deeply interesting conversation, and direct their attention to the food.

When they were driving back to Margaret's home, Nicholas said, "Nice couple! You're fortunate in your family, Meg. Will they be able to come up to town to dinner, do you think? Mother will want to hold an engagement party, I know."

Margaret was secretly appalled. "Oh, would that be absolutely necessary? I thought we'd just get engaged without any fuss and then, in due course, married quietly."

Nicholas didn't answer for several minutes, then he said, "I thought I remarked earlier that there was going to be no suspicion of anything sly about our engagement. Mother will want to give us a dinner party. We'll not be churlish enough to refuse, will we?"

Margaret knew she had been left with nothing to say.

She did not see Nicholas next day until she was putting her desk tidy prior to her lunch break. He walked into the office and said, "I've told Cook you won't be in to lunch today. I'm taking you out to lunch and then we're going to choose a ring."

With his remarks last night at her suggestion that they should dispense with an engagement ring still fresh in her mind, Margaret smiled and agreed. She fetched her hat and coat and they left the house together. They had a good lunch in a restaurant nearby and then took a taxi to a leading jeweller's and were ushered into the manager's office.

It was obvious that Nicholas had been here already

this morning, for the manager cleared his desk as soon as he saw him, and laying out a velvet cloth, he placed upon it eight rings.

Margaret drew in her breath when she saw them. Each was of a different stone, each perfect in its way. The settings too were different in each case, and she was quite bewildered when Nicholas invited her to try them on and make her choice.

The pearl and opal rings she immediately ruled out. She had never cared for either. But she timidly picked up the emerald, and slipped it on to her finger.

She held out her hand and admired it.

"Well," Nicholas inquired, "aren't you going to try the others?"

Margaret did so, one after the other, but she could not prevent her gaze wandering back to the emerald ring. It would probably clash with every garment she possessed, but she found it irresistible.

"That's settled, then," Nicholas said suddenly to the jeweller. "My fiancée likes the emerald."

"I didn't say so," Margaret exclaimed, startled.

Nicholas smiled mockingly. "You didn't need to, sweetheart, you hardly looked at the others."

He turned to the jeweller again. "Do you think it wants any alteration?"

The man picked up the ring and slipped it on to Margaret's ring finger.

"No, Mr. Hollis. It's an excellent fit. Any smaller and it would cause Madam discomfort."

"We shall want a wedding ring to match. Could we choose one now?"

The jeweller rang for a selection of wedding rings to be grought in. When they had chosen one, Nicholas wrote a cheque, and they went out into the street again. As Margaret reached the door, she stopped suddenly. "I've left my gloves," and she turned as if to go back into the shop.

Nicholas caught her arm. "No, I have them here. I picked them up when I saw you'd forgotten them."

He handed them to her as he spoke, and Margaret was chagrined to see that the careful mends she had done to one of the fingers was uppermost. Had he noticed? She sincerely hoped he hadn't . Mended gloves and large expensive emerald rings definitely did not go together.

In the taxi, as they returned to Chester Square, Margaret tried to thank him. Nicholas brushed her thanks aside almost brusquely and said, "If you like it, that's all that matters. An emerald suits you."

He picked up her left hand and studied it, then he smiled, almost shyly.

"I'm glad you chose that ring. It's the one I would have picked had it been left to me," and he kissed her hand swiftly before laying it in her lap.

Margaret was astonished. Somehow she had not connected such easy, affectionate ways with blunt Nicholas Hollis. And yet he had kissed her hand in the most natural manner, almost as if he had enjoyed making the gesture.

Jean was loud in her exclamations of envy when Margaret drove home with her sister the following evening. She had asked Nicholas to let her return home alone.

"My goodness, he's certainly done you proud, Margaret. I never saw a lovelier ring. Wait until I tell Clive. I've been hankering after a really nice dress ring for ages. If this baby turns out to be the daughter he so badly wants, I shall insist on a star sapphire at least." She chuckled. "Though it won't be in that class, I'm afraid. It's absolutely gorgeous. What did his mother say?"

"Mrs. Hollis liked our choice, I think." Margaret replied. "And that reminds me—she wants to give us an engagement party. Can you and Clive manage to come up for dinner next Saturday? I think you could fix a babysitter in the time, couldn't you? I shall want a bit of moral support, you know."

CHAPTER EIGHT

THE following morning, knowing that Mrs. Hollis had a morning appointment with her dressmaker, Mragaret had arranged with Mrs. Macgennis that they would do their periodic check of the household linen. They had just taken everything out of the big, roomy cupboard on the upper landing and were sorting it into piles, when Mrs. Hollis appeared at Margaret's elbow.

Margaret looked up in surprise. "Did you want me, Mrs. Hollis? I thought Mrs. Krol was coming at ten or I'd have come in to see you."

"Yes, I was expecting her, but she rang to say her husband isn't well and she'll be a little late. I wonder if you can come down when you and Nannie have finished, please? There's something I want to ask you."

Margaret looked at her employer across the pile of sheets she had been counting. "We may be some time. Shall I come right away?"

"Yes, perhaps that would be best," Mrs. Hollis answered absently. "Sorry, Nannie. I won't keep Margaret more than five minutes, I promise you."

As she followed her into the sitting-room, Margaret wondered if she had forgotten some important instruction. She had attended to everything she had thought was urgent before she had joined Mrs. Macgennis upstairs.

Mrs. Hollis sat down and waved Margaret to a chair. She began in her characteristically vague way. "Margaret, my dear, Mrs. Krol coming this morning has set me thinking. Your mother won't be able to help you choose your trousseau, will she?"

Margaret was puzzled. Lavish trousseaux were somewhat out of date and, in any case, quite beyond her slender means. She hadn't as yet given the matter much thought, but she would, she supposed, need some new clothes now she had become engaged. There were bound to be invitations from Nicholas's friends, and she had only the one dress which she had worn for the Hollis's dinner party.

As the thoughts jostled each other in her mind, Mrs. Hollis went on. "Well, perhaps not so much a trousseau, but I thought perhaps you might want some new things, especially for evening. I wondered, as your mother is in hospital and unable to advise you if you might let Mrs. Krol make some for you. It would be my little present to you."

Margaret stammered as she replied, "Oh, but—but, Mrs. Hollis. It's very kind of you, but . . ."

"That's settled, then, said Mrs. Hollis. "I'll let you know when Mrs. Krol gets here and we can put our heads together over what will suit you."

It was an obvious dismissal, and Margaret got up and went back to her sheets. Mrs. Krol was a little French-woman who had once worked for one of the big Paris fashion houses. She had met and married a Pole and they had settled in England after the end of the Second World War. When her husband had become too ill to work some years previously, Mrs. Krol had turned to her needle to bring in a little extra money to augment their pension. She was a very gifted needle-woman with all the French flair for making the simplest pattern and material into high fashion. Mrs. Hollis had discovered her many years before, and Margaret knew that anything she was fortunate enough to have made by little Mrs. Krol would be perfect.

It was with a half scared, half excited anticipation that she answered the summons later that day. She found her employer and the little dressmaker half hidden by a large pile of paper patterns and fashion magazines which littered the table. She was measured all over while Mrs. Krol wrote figures in tiny, sloping hand-writing in a little black notebook. When this was safely tucked away, she and Mrs. Hollis went into a long discussion from which Margaret was totally barred. Apart from the measuring glances in her direction she might have been invisible.

Mrs. Hollis seemed suddenly to notice Margaret's silence. She laughed suddenly. "Sorry, Margaret, but this is so thrilling. I've never had a daughter to dress. Will you leave it to Mrs. Krol and me? We thought cream lace in this pattern," and held out a design of a fairytale dress in delicate spider lace for Margaret to look at.

"It's beautiful, but . . ." Margaret wasn't allowed to finish.

"You like it—that's settled, then. Mrs. Krol will get on with it at once if it's to be ready for your engagement party. We can talk about the other things later."

Margaret had opened her mouth to remonstrate when Nicholas walked into the room. He stopped abruptly and said, "Sorry, am I interrupting?"

"No, come in Nicholas," his mother answered. "Have you met Mrs. Krol? She's come to see me about some new dresses."

"I suppose you're all absolutely exhausted, then," Nicholas suggested wickedly. "I've always understood choosing women's clothing is a very tiring business."

Mrs. Hollis smiled back at him, their faces for the moment looking almost ludicrously alike. "Quite the reverse. It's exhilarating. But you can take Margaret if you like. I think she's had enough."

As he closed the door behind them Nicholas said, "You look exhausted. Come along and have something to recuperate." He led the way to the library, and when Margaret was comfortably settled in a chair by the cheerful fire blazing in the grate, he went towards the array of bottles in the corner.

Margaret was holding out her hands towards the fire, but as he walked towards her, a glass in each hand, she sat up and took one from him. "What's the matter?" he asked abruptly. "Something worrying you?"

"It's your mother. She insists on making me a present of some new dresses. It's not right."

Nicholas raised his glass and said a brief "cheers" before he went on. "I don't see why you should mind. It will give Mother and enormous kick and I should have thought you'd have been delighted to have additions to your wardrobe. We'll be getting lots of invitations now, you know. All my friends will be wanting to look you over." He grinned mockingly. "You know what women are? If you turn up in the same dress more than twice. the tongues will wag like mad."

"Well, if your friends are so small minded that they're afraid to wear a dress more than twice in case everyone will gossip, I'm sorry for them," Margaret answered angrily.

"Now, don't get excited. I'm exaggerating, of course, but I can't believe you would really enjoy giving people the opportunity to criticize you. Say Blanche Miln-Prescott, for instance. She must have dozens of outfits, because I've never seen her in the same thing twice. In any case, meeting a lot of fresh faces is bound to be a bit of an ordeal and I should have thought a new frock or two would have given you a bit of confidence."

He watched her carefully as he finished speaking. Had he known it, he could not have said anything more likely to clinch the argument than his mention of Blanche Miln-Prescott. Margaret felt sure that the engagement would find no favour with that superior lady, and Nicholas was no fool. He had been quite right when he said a new frock gave women confidence. Margaret was going to need all her courage, she knew, when she faced Nicholas's circle of friends and acquaintances.

When she did not reply, but sat staring into her glass, Nicholas put one finger under Margaret's chin and tipped it up, so that she was forced to meet his eyes. His face was quite serious, the expression as usual inscrutable.

"Then that's settled, is it, sweetheart? No more heart-burning over accepting a few dresses?"

Margaret gazed back into his eyes, praying her ever-ready blush would not betray her. She gave a tiny sigh of relief as he released her and took out his cigarette case. Under that searching look she had been terrified that Nicholas would read her innermost thoughts.

Following the announcement of their engagement, Margaret and Nicholas each held a rather embarrassing interview, though neither confided in the other. Margaret had been busily engaged in sorting the morning's mail, when the telephone rang and the voice of William Pettigrew spoke in her ear.

"I say, old girl, you might have told me I'd be stepping on Nicholas Hollis's toes when I asked you out. Wasn't quite the thing, was it? You might have tipped me the wink that you were thinking of getting engaged."

Margaret was not only astonished but furious as well.

"I see no reason why I shouldn't have accepted your invitations," she replied, keeping her voice steady and non-committal with an effort. "I'd no idea I should be getting engaged and, in any case, you had no serious intentions. Now had you, William? Be honest! I was just a pleasant dinner companion."

However, Dr. Pettigrew was not to be so easily mollified, and he was still arguing in a resentful tone when Margaret, her patience at an end, put a stop to the conversation by excusing herself on the pretext of pressure of work. She sat looking at the telephone for several minutes before she recommenced sorting the letters, feeling a sick distaste at his attitude.

Her feeling of disquietude was increased later in the day by overhearing a little of the second conversation. She had just opened her door and was going upstairs with a parcel which had just been delivered for Mrs. Hollis when she was in time to see Blanche Miln-Prescott precipitate herself into the library, and apologetic Mrs. Macgennis immediately behind her. She heard Nicholas say, "All right, Mac," as through the open door Margaret saw Blanche slam down a newspaper on to the desk. As she went hastily upstairs she distinctly heard, "This can't be true! You can't possibly be going to marry that little ninny and make the same mistake again. She's just like Julie. You know she is."

At this point the voice died away, as to Margaret's great relief, Mrs. Macgennis closed the library door and went away. As she ran quickly up the stairs, she found herself trembling.

Inside the library, Blanche was still speaking. "That girl's as emotionally unstable as my dear little sister, and will probably end the same way."

By this time, Nicholas's face was white with anger.

"Are you sure you're being quite sensible to remind me of how Julie met her end, my dear Blanche? As I remember it, you had more than a hand in her emotional mixups, and it's not too late to resurrect the case. I still have that letter, you know."

"You wouldn't dare show it to anyone. Think of the scandal. And if you think I'd sit quietly and say nothing, you're quite wrong. I'd tell a pretty tale, believe me. Why can't you realize the inevitable, Nicholas? Marry me now, I've waited long enough." She came to an abrupt stop as she saw Nicholas was laughing.

"Marry *you*? My dear girl, if I were cast up on a desert island with you, I'd still not come near you. Can't you understand? You made a very successful hash of my first marriage, and you'd better think twice before you try and do anything to harm this one. Now get it firmly into your head that Margaret Grant and I are engaged. In about ten weeks we shall get married. Nothing and no one is going to prevent that. We are then going right away from your vicinity, but even if we weren't I wouldn't advise you to try and do anything to upset this marriage. If you do, I warn you that scandal or no scandal, I shall take that letter to some

136

of the interested parties. Your mother for one. Little though she liked Julie I can't believe she'd be a party to what was virtually her murder."

Blanche picked up her handbag, her eyes flashing dangerously. "What an exaggeration! Not a soul would believe you if you went around saying I'd murdered Julie. But I understand all right now. I believe you've fallen in love with that silly little thing!" and she almost ran out of the room, slamming the door to behind her.

Margaret thought long and seriously about the bit of conversation she had overheard. More than ever now she wondered what was between Blanche and Nicholas; could he have asked her to marry him merely to spite Blanche? She longed too to know more details of his first marriage. What had Julie really been like? He must, she thought, have been very much in love to have remained a widower for so long after her death. Or was it a case of a burnt child fearing the fire? The thoughts squirmed round and round in Margaret's head. She wished she could have asked Nicholas outright, but the thought of any such intimate conversation was, of course, out of the question. She could imagine the cold expression which would creep into his eyes if she were fool enough to ask him such a personal question.

When the evening of the engagement party arrived, Margaret was secretly relieved that she would be wearing a dress which could bear comparison with anything the other guests might be wearing. Mrs. Krol had exactly copied the picture of the beautiful cream lace dress Margaret had seen in the magazine. When she had slipped it over her head, she turned and looked herself over in the long mirror in her bedroom.

The dress fitted her slim figure perfectly. Margaret had managed to find evening shoes which were an exact match. The only colour was the flash of green fire from her engagement ring, and the warm glowing colour of her hair.

Clive and Jean were to call and take her up to town with them. When she was ready, Margaret put a dab of

137

perfume on her wrists, picked up her coat and handbag and went into the living-room to wait until they arrived. Jean was enchanted with her sister's dress. She, at least, had not seemed to share Margaret's reluctance about accepting the gifts of clothes from her future mother-in-law.

The evening passed off very successfully, Nicholas, to Margaret's relieved surprise, playing the part of a proud, possessive fiancé to perfection. If she were sceptical of the genuineness of his manner, at least it had the effect of protecting her from malicious remarks. Though Blanche Miln-Prescott and Mrs. Miln-Prescott were cool in their attitude towards her, at least they did nothing worse, and though Margaret caught Blanche glaring at her during the evening in anything but a friendly manner, at least she was spared any other examples of spitefulness.

The following day, Sunday, Nicholas and Margaret had arranged to drive down to see the matron of the nursing home in Bournemouth. It was raining when Nicholas called for her, but as the car sped towards the coast, the sun came out from behind a cloud, and the sunshine persisted until they reached the hotel where they were to have lunch.

When they arrived at the nursing home later that afternoon, there were a few minutes to spare before they were due for the appointment with the matron. Margaret left Nicholas smoking in the car while she went up to have a word with her mother's friend.

Mrs. Salmon was sitting in her large, comfortable room, enjoying the spring sunshine, which was flooding into it. "Margaret, my dear, how nice to see you. Matron said you were coming down today. Is your mother going to come here for her convalescence?"

"It's more than that, Aunt Mary," Margaret replied as she pulled up a small chair and sat down. "The doctor at the hospital doesn't seem to think Mother will improve any more than she has at present, and he feels she would be better living in a nursing home for good.

Jean and I would like her to come here—that is if we can arrange it. Mother won't like not living in her own home, but if she could be here with you, I think she wouldn't fret so much."

Mrs. Salmon nodded. "Yes, you're probably right." Then she nodded towards Margaret's left hand. "Before I forget, my dear, I see I'm to wish you happiness. When are you bringing the young man to visit me?"

Margaret smiled mischievously. "Today, if you like. He's outside now."

She rose as she spoke. "We'll come up again after seeing Matron if we shan't be disturbing your afternoon's rest."

Mrs. Salmon laughed. "Of course bring him up. I never take a rest in the accepted sense, Margaret. My life is one long rest!"

The matron received them in her living quarters, which were attached to the nursing home.

"Sorry to have to see you here, Miss Grant, but my office is being spring-cleaned, and I knew Sunday was the only day you could come down. Now, about your mother, I understand that you want her to become a permanent guest."

Margaret nodded. "Yes. I think I explained when I phoned that they hold out no hope at the hospital of Mother progressing any further, and they've recommended that she be put in a good nursing home. Of course, I immediately thought of you."

"Well, I'm afraid it's a little difficult," the matron explained. "We could have arranged for her to have the room next to her friend for a fortnight, but after that, it's booked for six months ahead. There is nothing else available."

Margaret's face fell. She looked at Nicholas for help. She had worried so about the fees, the thought that accommodation might not be available had never occurred to her.

"However," the matron continued, "I was talking to Mrs. Salmon this morning, and if you like, she says your mother can share her room until such time as we have a vacancy. As you know, Mrs. Salmon has a large corner room and we can easily move things around and fit in another bed."

Margaret blinked rapidly. "How very kind. If Mrs. Salmon has really suggested that herself, I couldn't be more grateful. Mother would like it enormously, I know."

Arrangements were then rapidly completed for Mrs. Grant to move down in ten days' time, and Nicholas gave the name of his solicitors, and instructed the matron to forward the accounts to them for settlement.

Afterwards they went back upstairs again to have tea with Mrs. Salmon. After introducing Nicholas, Margaret hugged the old lady to her. "You are a darling, Aunt Mary, offering to share your room with Mother. Thank you very much," and she kissed her cheek.

Mrs. Salmon looked up at Nicholas, who was lounging in the window.

"Margaret is thanking me for doing myself a favour. Mrs. Grant and I have known each other since schooldays, and we've always a lot to talk about. I haven't talked in bed after 'lights out' for years," she added meditatively. Margaret and Nicholas both laughed at her pensive tone, and the remainder of the afternoon passed in the most amicable manner, Nicholas obviously setting himself out to be entertaining.

When they left at five-thirty it looked like rain again and was already beginning to get dusk. The skies were overcast, and though the rain held off, it was a damp and blustery wind which greeted them as they walked down to have a look at the sea.

Margaret tied a scarf over her hair and turned up the collar of her coat.

"Too cold?" Nicholas inquired.

"No, but it's a bit chilly after the warmth in the nursing home," Margaret answered.

"Feel like a short walk before dinner? I've ordered

it for seven o'clock. We don't want to be too late back."

Margaret nodded, and Nicholas at once tucked his hand in her arm and walked her off down the promenade. There were not many people about, and they had an enjoyable hour's walk before returning to the warmth and comfort of the hotel.

Margaret's cheeks were glowing as she walked into the foyer, and more than one pair of masculine eyes turned interestedly upon her as she took off her scarf and shook her hair into place.

Nicholas frowned. "Meet me in the bar in fifteen minutes," he said in his usual abrupt manner, and walked off.

It was fully twenty minutes later, however, when Margaret had washed and redone her face, and tidied her hair. She walked into the bar and found Nicholas sitting on a stool, talking to the elderly barman. Two glasses were standing already filled on the counter before him, and Margaret smiled to herself.

"Engaged only four days," she was thinking, "and already he orders without asking my preferences. Now is that because he thinks I know very little about drinks, or because he thinks he knows what's good for me?"

She didn't realize that it would not take a magician to guess what she had been thinking. Nicholas had looked up in time to see her glance at the glasses and then the small smile twitch her mouth. He grinned sardonically but said nothing. He put one of the glasses into her hand and raising the other murmured a solemn "To us!"

Margaret smiled back, but didn't reply. She raised her own glass and sipped at its contents.

"Um, very good! You remembered I like dry sherry?"

The smile died, the eyebrows were raised. "Of course. Did you think I'd forget?"

"Oh, goodness," Margaret thought, "I wish I hadn't said that. Is he going to be difficult now? We've had such a lovely day so far."

But her fears were not realized. As if he had somehow detected her feelings of apprehension, Nicholas behaved with perfectly good manners towards her until it was time to begin their journey home.

The weather had worsened again by nine o'clock and the wind was blowing almost at gale force. As they reached the New Forest, rain began to fall heavily, and once or twice the car skidded as it was hit by the huge gusts of wind.

Margaret glanced at Nicholas the second time this happened, though she did not speak. He was staring grimly ahead, grasping the wheel in strong, capable hands. He lessened his speed, but on the next bend the car skidded even more violently as it hit a patch of mud and wet leaves, and the next moment, despite Nicholas wrenching at the wheel in the hope of correcting the skid, they slid almost gently off the road and down into a shallow ditch.

When the car finally came to rest, Nicholas had fallen heavily on to Margaret, despite his grasp on the wheel, since her side was underneath. He put his hand out, and grasping the door handle, managed to pull himself away.

"Have I hurt you, Meg?" he asked.

Margaret rubbed her left arm where it had hit the door.

"No. I've only bruised my arm. Are you all right?"

"Of course. I fell soft," and he smiled mockingly as he commenced trying to open the offside door. It stuck for a moment or two, but when he exerted more pressure it flew open, letting in a flurry of wind and rain.

"You stay here. I'll go and try to stop a car. We can't stay here all night and we shall need some sort of breakdown vehicle to get us out, I think."

He got out as he spoke and gently shut the door. The headlights were still burning, and by their light Margaret was able to see Nicholas reach the road and look first to the left and then to his right. He strode off and the minutes ticked by.

142

Suddenly he materialized again beside the car and opened the door.

"I've stopped a farm worker. He's only driving a Land Rover, but he says he'll take us into Lyndhurst. I think we should accept his offer. The rain is getting worse and I want to get you under cover."

Margaret put up her hands and Nicholas pulled her out of the car. They ran together up the bank and Margaret climbed in beside the young man holding open the door to the Land Rover. Nicholas got in behind, and they set off.

It wasn't a very comfortable journey. There were no side screens and the wind and rain blew in remorselessly. Margaret breathed a sigh of relief when the lights of habitation again loomed up.

The young countryman set them down at the door of a large inn, and after a few words of thanks, Nicholas hurried her inside. They stood in the warmth and comfort and surveyed each other ruefully.

Despite the fact that she had turned up the collar of her coat and worn a headscarf, Margaret knew she was both wet and windblown. Nicholas was wearing no hat, and his hair and face were wet with rain.

"I think we'd better see if they can put us up tonight. They'll not get the car out and fixed before tomorrow, and the sooner you're in a hot bath, the better. Otherwise you'll be in for a chill."

Nicholas removed his wet overcoat as he spoke and turned to the reception desk. A few minutes later he came back to Margaret. She was trying to dry her face on a small handkerchief, and he handed her a large one, with a faint grin.

"They've got a couple of rooms, and they're going to ring a garage for me. You go up. I'll have something hot sent up to you."

Margaret followed the neat maid who by this time had appeared to show her the way to her room. It was a large room with a big comfortable-looking double bed, and she discovered that the bathroom was next door. Margaret lost no time in running the steaming hot water into the bath.

She had just returned to her room some twenty minutes later, when a knock fell on the door. She was wearing only her slip, so she quickly picked up her coat which had dried on the bathroom radiator while she had been soaking in the hot water. Thinking it would be either the maid or a waiter with the promised hot drink, Margaret buttoned up the coat and opened the door and peeped out.

Nicholas stood outside, a tray in his hands containing a plate of sandwiches and two steaming glasses. He walked in and put the tray down on the table.

As Margaret closed the door he asked, "Had a hot bath?"

"Yes. I've just finished," Margaret nodded.

"Get into bed, then. It's warm in here, but I don't want you catching cold."

Margaret laughed shakily. "I don't catch cold easily, you know," but she padded over to the bed in her bare feet and climbed in. She continued, "It's you who should be getting a hot bath, not me. You're the one who has had two doses of 'flu this winter."

Nicholas grinned as he came over and put one of the glasses on the bedside table. "Never mind about me. A couple of these hot toddies, and no self-respecting germ will come near me. Here you are, infant. Get that down." He took a sip from his own glass. "What a fool I was to skid off the road like that! However, the garage I rang are going to pick the car up right away, and it will be ready, they say, by eight-thirty in the morning, so we should be able to make an early start."

He started to eat a sandwich as he finished speaking, then suddenly realizing that he had not offered the plate to Margaret, he picked it up and walked towards the bed. She was sipping gratefully at the hot, spicy contents of her glass. Putting it down, she took a sandwich and sat nibbling it.

Margaret's hair, damp from the rain and the steam

144

of the bath, curled in wild disorder about her head. Nicholas sat down on the end of the bed and surveyed her.

"You look about fourteen," he said after a moment, with his usual candour. "In fact, after a surfeit of sophisticated women, you are the most perfect contrast."

Margaret did her best to control the usual ready blush. "I hoped I looked very sophisticated last night," she remarked, in an endeavour to lead his attention away from her present state of scrubbed, shiny face, and untidy hair.

"Oh, you did! I was quite frightened of you. For a moment I thought the wrong girl had come to dinner," he said mockingly. Then as the blush really got the better of her, and her face flamed, he laughed and said, "No more chatter. Finish your drink and settle down. I've ordered breakfast to be brought up to you at half past seven. Good night now!" and he got up and sauntered out of the room.

Margaret finished her sandwich, torn between conflicting emotions of wishing he had stayed, and relief that he had gone before he had made any more embarrassing comments on her appearance.

They were on the road for London again next morning promptly by eight-thirty. They made good time and by half past ten Margaret was at her desk.

The following week, Mrs. Grant was taken down to Bournemouth by ambulance and installed in her friend's room at the nursing home. The matron had most skilfully rearranged things so that the two ladies did not feel overcrowded, and when Margaret and Jean drove home that evening, both were more than satisfied that their mother would be happy in her new surroundings.

"By the way, when's the wedding?" Jean asked, as she drove up the London road. "I hope you're going to wait until after June. I should just hate to miss it, and I shan't want to appear looking extremely matronly."

Margaret hesitated for a moment before replying.

"Nothing definite has been fixed," she said at last, "but it won't be before June, I'm sure."

Jean glanced briefly at her sister, but Margaret was gazing straight ahead and did not notice the keen look which her sister had directed at her.

Following her mother's departure for the nursing home, Margaret began to feel as if she were on some sort of helter-skelter. She had thought she would have a great deal more spare time now she no longer needed to go in to see her mother every evening, but she and Nicholas received so many invitations from his relations and friends to join parties for dinner, for the theatre and other entertainments that life began to assume all the aspects of an endless attempt to cram twenty-five hours' activity into twenty-four. On several occasions there had been no time to go home and change in the evenings, and Mrs. Hollis had suggested that Margaret keep sufficient things there so that when necessary she and Nicholas could go on to evening engagements without the delay involved in her going home to change.

However, without fail, she spent each Sunday in Bournemouth, often being run down by Nicholas himself, but sometimes going alone on the train. She began to look forward to these Sundays without his company, since it gave her a breathing space to try and get her thoughts into perspective.

Though they now spent so much time in each other's company, Margaret still found Nicholas as inscrutable as ever. What he thought was a closed book to her, unless, on very rare occasions, he opened up to her. The only comforting thought she took to bed with her these days, was the discovery that they shared the same sense of humour and the same sense of the ridiculous. On several occasions, something had happened which had amused Margaret very much, and she had looked up to see Nicholas gazing across a dinner table or a crowded room at her, a precise appreciation of the situation apparent in his eyes.

Apart from this, they seemed to her to be like two well-

146

reharsed, well-behaved people carry out an elaborate charade. Nicholas himself made no move towards a warmer relationship, and so Margaret was careful to give him no indication of the state of her own emotions. He kissed her lightly, when circumstances demanded it, but when they parted at night, as often as not he simply gave her a brief wave before driving away. Margaret often found it difficult not to give herself away. On one occasion as he had kissed her lightly on the cheek, it was as much as she could do to prevent herself turning her head and giving him her lips instead.

Though she was careful to wear plenty of make-up to disguise her pallor she could not conceal the fact that she was losing weight. Once or twice Jean had seemed on the point of asking questions, but had evidently thought better of it and turned the conversation into other channels. However, as the weather got warmer, and summer seemed really to be at hand at last, Margaret noticed that occasionally Nicholas quite naturally began to behave like a conventional fiancé. It was almost as if at last he had decided to let his guard down. Margaret could not understand what had brought about the change, but was not prepared to ruin things by asking questions.

However, matters came to a head one week-end early in June. It had been a glorious week, and on the Friday Nicholas suggested that they go down to Bournemouth for the entire week-end, starting out as soon as Margaret had finished work on Friday afternoon.

London had been hot, the flat looked depressingly in need of a thorough cleaning, and Margaret herself not at all in the mood to tackle it. Through her conscience pricked her, she agreed, and before she could change her mind, Nicholas had fixed hotel rooms, times of departure and all other details.

When it was time to leave, Margaret was glad she was not returning to clean a stuffy flat as she had planned. I'll ask Mrs. Willis to give me a hand next week-end, she thought as she got into the car.

As they sped towards the outskirts of London and the green countryside, Margaret gave a long sigh of contentment. Nicholas glanced sideways.

"Hot, wasn't it? It will be nice to see the sea and feel a cool breeze. We don't need to go up and see your mother tonight, do we?"

"No, she's not expecting me until tomorrow. I'll go first thing in the morning."

They spoke little on the way down and arrived in good time for dinner. Nicholas had booked in at one of the larger hotels, and Margaret was glad she had packed one of her new dinner dresses. After a quick bath, she changed and went downstairs to find Nicholas awaiting her in the bar. He smiled warmly at her as he handed her a glass and raised his own in a silent toast.

When they had finished their drinks, they went into the dining-room and ordered. Margaret looked around her. The hotel was, it seemed, well filled, since few, if any, of the tables were unoccupied. The dining-room was full of the usual crowd to be found at such places, and Margaret caught herself giving a small sigh as she turned her attention back to Nicholas. She was just in time to see the wine waiter offer a gold-topped bottle for his inspection.

"Champagne?" Margaret's voice held surprise. "What are we celebrating?"

"Having tonight to ourselves," he replied promptly. "I find I can't remember one evening lately when we haven't either been to a party, or out with a party or getting dragged off with a party somewhere or other. Since it's quite an event to be on our own, I thought we'd mark the occasion. Do you mind?" Both brows went up in his typical way as if he were challenging Margaret to oppose him.

"No, I don't mind. In fact, I'm all for it," said Margaret. "Champagne always makes all my troubles seem very small."

"Troubles, my sweet? I thought I'd relieved you of

148

most of those. Now—tell me. What other troubles have you got? Maybe I could relieve you of them all."

He reached over and laid his hand over hers as he spoke. Margaret was so taken aback that she could not answer for a moment, and when she had summoned her voice the waiter had returned with their first course. Nicholas quickly withdrew his hand and shook out his table napkin.

He didn't resume the interrupted conversation until coffee had been brought. As he lighted Margaret's cigarette, his eyes met and held her own.

"Now! Let's be knowing about these other troubles you have."

He lit his own cigarette and sat waiting. Margaret exhaled slowly. How could she tell this difficult, enigmatic man that the biggest and most overwhelming trouble she had was that she was head over heels in love with him, and was terrified in case he should guess?

With an effort she looked away from the grey eyes regarding her so steadily, and carefully tapped ash off her cigarette. A few minutes more looking at her and he wouldn't need to be told anything. It would all be written clearly on her face.

"Well," he prodded her, "aren't you going to tell me?"

Margaret looked up and managed a convincing laugh. "Troubles to a woman are usually a combination of a lot of niggling pinpricks that a man wouldn't even call a trouble, you know. Do you really want to be bothered with a lot of feminine neuroses?"

Nicholas continued to look at her in silence for a moment or two, quietly smoking his cigarette. Margaret was beginning to find the smile on her face becoming something of a strain when he spoke.

"What you really mean, Meg, is that you have no intention of telling me what's worrying you. Put very tactfully, of course. Never mind! I'll find out some time."

He stood up as he spoke. "Finished? Then let's go

and have some fresh air for half an hour or so, shall we?"

"Yes, I'd love that. Wait until I get a coat, will you?"

Margaret went quickly up to her room, repaired her make-up and picked up the light coat she had brought with her. She ran downstairs to find Nicholas outside the swing doors, waiting for her. Her arm tucked in his, they set off.

Threequarters of an hour later found them on the cliffs, facing the on-shore breeze. Margaret had been gazing out to sea letting the hair blow back off her face, when something made her turn and look at Nicholas.

He was watching her, his usual unreadable expression for once absent from the grey eyes looking into hers. Margaret, who had been saying how lucky they were to be able to escape from the hot stuffiness of town, stopped in mid-sentence. She stayed there, her lips still parted, and gazed back, the sherry brown eyes widening as Nicholas reached out and drew her against him.

She stiffened momentarily as his lips met hers. Then the instinctive resistance went out of her, and she responded warmly to his kiss. Eyes closed, Margaret wondered if her legs would ever be able to carry her again. By the time Nicholas raised his head and released her, they felt as if they were made of India-rubber.

He laughed and said, "The last time we kissed like that, I owed it all to Pimms. Let's go and have another and see what you do after Pimms *and* champagne," and he turned and marched her briskly back towards the hotel.

When they got back to the hotel, it was to find dancing in progress and the hotel packed with people. Nicholas, however, managed to find a small table conveniently tucked away from the crowd, from where they could watch the dancers.

Here they sat smoking and talking, sipping the ice-cold drinks the busy waiter had quickly brought them, until Nicholas caught Margaret in the middle of stifling a yawn.

He immediately stubbed out his cigarette and rose to his feet. He held out a hand. "Come along, Meg. Bed! You're tired," and they collected their keys and entered the lift.

Margaret both feared and hoped alternately as they walked down her corridor, but Nicholas with a "sleep well, my love", and a very brief brush of the lips on her cheek, left her at her bedroom door.

Next morning, they both went round and surprised Mrs. Grant early. They sat and talked until shooed out by the nurses serving lunches, returning in the afternoon, when Mrs. Grant had awakened from her afternoon nap.

Nicholas was at his most amusing, keeping both Mrs. Grant and Mrs. Salmon, as well as any of the nursing staff who had occasion to come into the room, in gales of laughter. It was a side of himself he rarely showed, and Margaret was content to sit quietly and enjoy this unusual mood he was in.

He looked very young as he talked, and Margaret had an insight into the eager young man he must have been before circumstances marked the lines on his face, and put the hardness in his yes. Now, his whole face was lit with fun as he told a particularly far-fetched story about what life had been like for a very new National Serviceman. That her mother and Mrs. Salmon were enjoying themselves was plain to be seen.

They finally left the nursing home at six o'clock and returned to the hotel. As they were going up in the lift, Nicholas said suddenly, 'Shall we drive out and have dinner at some smaller place? If last night is anything to go by, this place will be too overcrowded for comfort in a couple of hours."

Margaret turned a smiling face. "Oh, yes, please! I don't think I want to stay in a big crowd all evening. It's too lovely an evening to be in a hot, noisy hotel."

When Margaret finally came downstairs, the green chiffon dress bringing out the fire of her engagement ring,

151

Nicholas was waiting with the car at the door. They drove out of Bournemouth, and took the road north.

"I was talking to the manager while I was waiting," Nicholas said. "He told me about a little place somewhere along this road. We have to turn left about ten miles out. He said there's a sign on the left-hand side of the road of a golden stag. Think you can spot it?"

He and Margaret both saw the sign simultaneously, however, and Nicholas swung the car into the small secondary road. About a mile and a half further along, another sign pointed to yet a smaller lane, and there stood a beautiful old timbered inn.

Only about half a dozen cars stood in the small yard, and when Nicholas and Margaret entered the inn, the owner greeted them by name.

"Mr. Hollis? Nicholas nodded. "My friend"—the landlord mentioned the name of the manager of their hotel in Bournemouth—"rang to tell me you were coming, and I've reserved a table for you. Would you like a drink first, or would you like to go straight into the dining-room?"

They said they would have a drink first and were ushered into the tiny saloon bar. Margaret looked around her with interest. The interior of the inn was as carefully preserved as the outside, and whoever had done the decorations and furnishings must have had a considerable knowledge of antiques and period tastes. However, they had not kept strictly to the discomforts of some of the period pieces, and modern inventions had been incorporated to make one of the most charming rooms Margaret had ever seen.

When they had drunk their sherries, Margaret and Nicholas went into the small dining-room. There were only about eight or nine tables, each laid, Margaret noticed, with dinner mats, well-polished cutlery and gleaming glassware. In the centre of each table was a small bowl of cottage flowers.

They were led to a table beside the window. This opened on to a brick-covered terrace, with a low parapet, since the ground level dropped abruptly immediately behind the house.

When the menu was brought, Margaret chose hors-d'oeuvres from a lavish selection wheeled to their table on a trolley, followed by a mouth-melting steak accompanied by cream spinach, beans and button potatoes. Nicholas seconded her choice and ordered a mellow wine to accompany their meal.

When they finally reached the coffee stage, Margaret felt replete and at peace, a state she concluded to be the aftermath of too much good food and wine. As they wandered outside and sat on the parapet to look at the view, it was beginning to get dusk. Nicholas lighted one of the small cigars he sometimes smoked in preference to cigarettes, and teasingly offered her one.

Margaret laughed up at him as she refused. She accepted a cigarette, however, and they sat in silence looking out on the peaceful countryside. Across the small valley, the lights were beginning to come on, one by one.

Suddenly, Margaret became aware that Nicholas had turned and was watching her, but when she looked inquiringly at him, he only asked if she would like a drink.

"Oh, I don't think I could," she said laughingly, her hand pressed to the waistline of her frock.

"Mind if I have a beer, then?" and when she shook her head, he sauntered in through the lighted door of the inn.

Margaret sat on alone, wishing that life could always be as peaceful and as uncomplicated as this. How different Nicholas had been all week-end. They might almost have been a normaly engaged couple.

Next day, the weather gave every indication of being as hot as ever. They sat with Margaret's mother during the morning, but as they were leaving at lunchtime, she asked them not to come back until five o'clock.

"Go and have a bathe or something, my dears. It's much too nice a day to sit indoors with two old cronies."

Nicholas looked across the room at Margaret. "Would you like a swim this afternoon?" he asked.

"Yes, I would. Are you sure you wouldn't mind, Mother?"

Mrs. Grant reassured them, and promising to return in time for tea at the nursing home, they left to have a quick lunch. Then collecting their things, they went down to the beach.

Nicholas hired a gaudy beach umbrella, and they found a deserted corner and settled down on the warm sand. Margaret took off the cotton frock she was wearing and sat, in her black one-piece bathing suit, watching the sea.

"I suppose we daren't go in until lunch has settled," she remarked.

Nicholas was already lying full length on his stomach, his face buried in his arms. He looked up, however, to smile and say, "I'm feeling far too lazy to go in yet in any case. Lie down, Meg, and have a few minutes' relaxation."

Margaret did so, thinking how much broader and stronger he looked stripped down to a pair of brief swimming trunks. She had always thought of Nicholas as a slightly built man, but the width of the brown shoulders besides her, almost touching her own, were a revelation. How deceptive good tailoring can be, she thought wryly, as she shut her eyes.

Lying there, enjoying the warmth of the sun, the soothing sound of the waves breaking on the sand, Margaret did not know at what moment she drifted off into a light sleep. She knew what awakened her, though. She lay with her eyes still closed, savouring the light kisses being pressed on her ear and cheek.

When she opened her eyes, Nicholas gave her ear one last kiss, and then looked up with a faint grin.

"Hm, you smell nice! A special English smell of fresh air, plenty of soap and roses."

Margaret's mouth curved up at the corners. "How am I to take that?"

His murmur was very soft. "Any way you choose. Though it was meant as a compliment," and his mouth moved slowly across her cheek until his lips found hers.

Margaret couldn't have helped herself. Almost without her own volition, her arms went round him, enjoying the feel of the smooth, warm skin beneath her hands. She was so lost in the magic of that kiss that she did not know when his hand left her shoulder, and moving downwards, began gently to caress her.

Startled, more by her own eager participation in this embrace, Margaret wrenched her mouth away from his and sat up abruptly, so abruptly that she took Nicholas by surprise. As he fell back on to the sand she got swiftly to her feet, and snatching up her bathing cap, ran down to the water's edge.

She plunged straight into the sea, the first embrace of the cold water on her body making her gasp. She swam out until her arms began to tire before turning prudently shorewards again.

Margaret could not pick out Nicholas from the other men on the beach until he sauntered down to the water, smoking a cigarette. He stood in the shallows until he had finished it, and then dived into the sea himself, but he did not swim towards her.

The rest of the afternoon passed in a haze of misery for Margaret. Though she tried to behave as usual, she found herself chattering and laughing in what was almost an hysterical manner, and she thought her mother would be sure to notice. However, Mrs. Grant, whatever her observations, made no comment, and it was not until they were on their way back to London that Margaret's feverish manner dropped from her and she relapsed into silence. A silence which Nicholas, who had been at his most dour, did nothing to break.

To her surprise, he got out of the car and accompanied her into the flat when they reached Bromley. He interrupted her nervous offer of a drink by going and putting the kettle on and himself making a cup of tea for them both.

When the tea had been poured, Nicholas produced his case and lit two cigarettes. Seating himself on the edge of the table, he picked up his cup and sat sipping the hot liquid slowly and watching Margaret over the rim of his cup.

When he did finally speak, he surprised her.

"Do you never feel like relaxing and letting yourself drift with the tide sometimes, Meg? You're always on your guard. It must have been a difficult time for you these past years, and particularly hard for a girl of your temperament."

"Of my temperament? What do you mean?"

"Well, despite your efforts to prove me wrong, you are a very normal girl, aren't you?"

"Normal? In what way? Decency?" Margaret was beginning to lose her temper.

"That too, of course, but you know that wasn't what I meant," said Nicholas. "I meant . . ." he broke off and grinned wickedly. "Perhaps I could show you what I mean."

"If it has anything to do with what happened this afternoon, don't bother. I know perfectly well how normal I am. You mustn't do that again."

As soon as the words were out, Margaret realized her mistake. One of his eyebrows rose.

"Mustn't? Don't you know, Meg, that's a fighting word where I come from?" and he advanced towards her.

Margaret backed away from him until she was stopped by the dresser behind her. Despite her struggles, Nicholas took her firmly into his arms. His eyes were alight now with what to Margaret seemed a positively diabolical mirth.

When she was a helpless prisoner, he smiled into her eyes and said, "So you're quite normal and you know your own temperament perfectly. And you definitely don't want to do *this*."

His lips covered hers as he spoke. The kiss was infinitely gentle, infinitely beguiling, and Margaret immediately stopped trying to twist her face away from his and closing her eyes slipped her arms round his waist.

Abruptly he let her go and stood back, so abruptly that if Margaret had not grasped the hard edges of the dresser, she would have fallen.

Then with a murmured, "See what I mean!" he walked out of the kitchen and out of the house. She knew exactly what he had meant now. It was all she could do not to call him to come back.

CHAPTER NINE

For some time after he had left, Margaret did not move. She simply stood, holding on to the dresser, while the tears slipped down her flushed cheeks.

"I wouldn't mind," she whispered to the empty room, to the half-smoked cigarette he had left still burning in the ashtray on the table. "I wouldn't mind if he loved me, but it's just a game to him," and the tears fell faster, until she was blinded by them.

But Margaret was eminently normal, as she had boasted, and too sensible to cry for long over something she felt she could not alter. Taking a handkerchief out of her coat pocket, she blew her nose, wiped her eyes and went to prepare for bed.

Next day, she did not see Nicholas, nor did he ring her when she went home after the day's work. During the day, Mrs. Hollis had surprised her by suggesting they begin advertising for her replacement, "For, my dear, it's only a few weeks now to the wedding and I'd like you to train someone to be as good as yourself, if possible. I'm going to miss you when you go," she went on. Then, with a faint smile, she added, "If Nicholas were not my son, I'd never forgive him for stealing you away!"

When Margaret went down to phone the proposed advertisement to two of the daily newspapers, she wondered if, in fact, Mrs. Hollis would really be losing her. Somehow the actual wedding remained such a nebulous figment of her imagination, it seemed too improbable to be real.

On Tuesday morning, Nicholas walked into the office before Margaret had even removed her outdoor things. One glance at his face told her that the mood of the weekend was as if it had never been. His features were as expressionless as usual, his eyes, when he did look directly at her, held a sardonic gleam which filled her with apprehension.

However, whatever unpleasant things he might have intended to do or say, Margaret was not to know, for as he started to speak the phone rang. Murmuring an excuse, Margaret lifted the receiver.

"That you, Margaret?" her brother-in-law's voice said. "Guess what? You've another bouncing nephew."

Margaret was startled. "But I thought it wasn't due for another three weeks."

"Nor it was, but Jean jumped the gun. Anyway, it's all over, and I've just left Jean at the maternity home very pleased with herself, and congratulating herself on her slim figure again."

He laughed as he spoke. "That's not the only reason I rang. Margaret, can you help me out? I know you're pretty heavily committed, but this urgency of my offspring to arrive has rather put our arrangements out. The boys can be collected after nursery school at lunchtime by a neighbour who will look after them until around five, but then she's got to go and cope with her own family. Can you possibly take over after that, at least until I can fix something else? Will Hollis cut up rough or anything?"

Margaret looked across at Nicholas, a determined light in her eyes. "Don't worry about that, Clive. Of course I can cope. I'll be there to take the twins over

158

this afternoon, and I'll stay at night. That is, if you are agreeable?"

"Good girl! I knew you'd manage. Must dash now. See you this evening, then!" and he rang off.

Margaret replaced the receiver.

"That was my brother-in-law. Jean has had another boy."

"Good for her! They want you to give a hand with the children, I suppose?"

"Yes—Jean wasn't supposed to be having this baby for another three weeks. It's thrown out all their plans. I'll have to look after the boys each night until she comes out of hospital. Will it be a frightful nuisance to you? I know we'd said we would dine with the Christie's tomorrow, and then there's that charity ball on the fifteenth. You've got the tickets, haven't you?"

"Don't worry about that. And I'll explain to the Christies. They'll understand," and he sauntered out of the room.

As Margaret hung up her coat, she wondered what he had originally come in to say to her. Whatever it had been, her domestic problem must have put it out of his mind. Or he had decided not to bother.

However, the morning's work crowded in, and she dismissed Nicholas from her mind. Shortly before she was due to leave at five o'clock he strode quickly into her office.

"I can't manage to run you down, Meg, so I've arranged for a taxi to come for you here in fifteen minutes. It will come at the same time every night until your sister is home. Then in case I'm tied up, like tonight, you can get there quickly."

Margaret was touched by his thoughtfulness. She looked across at him. "It's very good of you, Nicholas. You didn't have to bother, you know. I could have gone on the train."

"Yes, and if I know you, you'd have worried yourself sick in case you were five minutes late getting down to your precious nephews." He smiled faintly at her. "Do you go in for lame dogs, as well as being general call-boy to your family, by any chance?"

"Oh, I'm not!" Margaret exclaimed indignantly, all the charity she had been feeling towards him ebbing rapidly. "In any case, I like helping people if I can."

"Yes, I know." He grinned now openly. "Don't think I mind. I just want to be forewarned so I know what to expect when we're married," and before Margaret could think up a fitting retort, he had strolled out of the room.

When Margaret stepped out of the taxi at her sister's home, the front door flew open and the twins raced down the path. Her hair was all over the place and she had lost one glove before they were satisfied she had been adequately welcomed.

By the time a grinning taxi-driver had retrieved her belongings and had handed them to her, the neighbour who had been minding the boys had come to the gate, dressed in her outdoor things.

"You must be Miss Grant. Paul and Keith have been very good. I'll pick them up at the nursery at the same time tomorrow," and she waved good-bye before Margaret had time to do more than say a very brief "thank you".

Paul and Keith hung on her arms, both talking at once.

"Do you know Mummy has gone to fetch our new baby brother, Auntie Margaret? He's got no teeth, Daddy says, and he can't walk. *And* he's bald. Fancy being bald! We've got lots of hair and teeth. Why hasn't he?"

As Margaret removed her coat, she tried to explain to two excited little boys why babies came without all the etceteras, but before she was half-way through the explanation, they had gone on to something else.

"Daddy says he's going to be called David. Do you like the name David, Auntie Margaret? We wanted him to be called Sydney. We always call our caterpillars Sydney. And if he can't walk, he must be like a caterpillar and can only crawl."

Margaret giggled, and when they saw her face break into smiles, the twins laughed with her. I can't, she thought, explain to them that the baby won't even crawl. They'll be too disgusted; so she hugged them to her and said, "Never mind, poppets. Perhaps Mummy and Daddy will call him David Sydney, then you'll all be satisfied."

By the time Clive came home from the maternity hospital a few minutes before eight, the boys had been fed, bathed, read to, and were sound asleep. Margaret was just dishing up an appetising meal.

While he ate, she sat down and plied her brother-in-law with questions. He put down his knife and fork and laughed lightheartedly. "Oh, you women! A new baby gets you all, doesn't it? I had to go through a positive catechism from Mother before I left the office. She won't be satisfied that we've produced another as good, if not better, than the twins until she's seen him with her own eyes. Thank heaven she's going in to see Jean for herself tomorrow."

Margaret laughed with him as she started to clear away.

"And talking of women loving another new baby," she inquired, "I forgot to ask. Have you let Mother know?"

"Good lord, yes. First thing Jean said when I saw her this morning. I telephoned to the matron and she said she'd give your mother a message. I know she's heard because there was a huge bouquet of flowers from her and Mrs. Salmon when I got round to see Jean this evening."

When Margaret arrived at the office next morning, she found they had received a great many answers to the advertisement. Mrs. Hollis looked through the applications and asked Margaret to write to six of the girls to come for an interview.

As she typed these notes and sent off short replies to

those Mrs. Hollis did not think would suit her. Margaret wondered idly what her successor would be like. That is, if she did eventually marry Nicholas. The engagement still held for her all the unrealities of a play in which she had been cast for one of the principal parts.

That evening, when she arrived at her sister's home, the baby-sitter told her that the twins had had a nap during the afternoon.

I know what that means, thought Margaret, as she hugged her exuberant nephews, they certainly won't be ready for bed at six-thirty.

Their excessive high spirits confirmed her worst fears, so she looked out two aprons and tying them round two fat tummies, she took the boys into the kitchen and gave them a piece of pastry dough to play with while she set about filling her sister's cake tins. She quickly made a big chocolate sponge, and since the twins were still happily engaged with two pieces of now dirty grey dough, she made two big apple pies and two flan cases which could be filled later.

She had just put the pastry into the oven and was engaged in gently turning the halves of the sponge on to a wire cooler, when the back door opened quietly behind her.

Margaret looked over her shoulder, straight into a pair of laughing grey eyes. She coloured. "I didn't expect you." Even to herself, the tone sounded unusually abrupt.

"Well, you might at least pretend you were pleased to see me," Nicholas said, as he kissed her cheek.

The boys were standing transfixed, their eyes on his face. Though they had seen him now on several occasions, they were still a bit in awe of this man who usually came in order to carry away their beloved Auntie Margaret. This time he looked as if he had come to stay. He carried a laden shopping basket in one hand, and the pockets of his jacket bulged with mysterious packets.

"Hello, you chaps. Helping your Auntie Meg, are you?" Nicholas greeted them. "In that case, you won't have time to help me unpack."

With one accord, pastry was abandoned in favour of this new diversion.

"For goodness' sake, Nicholas, make them wash their hands first. They were clean half an hour ago, but look at them now. You'll be covered with flour."

But it was too late. Already four sticky hands had plunged into his two outside pockets, and sweets, balloons, whistles and dinky toys were produced and, had Nicholas not quickly prevented it, spread across the kitchen table between cakes, pastry and all the other cooking impedimenta.

Margaret couldn't help laughing as he quickly tried to retrieve things from the twins' quick fingers. She grabbed Paul and took him over to the sink. After washing and drying him and his twin, she told them to take everything into the living-room.

A few minutes later, Nicholas sauntered back into the kitchen. He had shed his jacket and there was a wide grin on his face.

"Couple of rare devils, those two, aren't they?" he said conversationally as he watched Margaret make a filling of sugar, ground almonds, cocoa and a spoonful of coffee. She spread it on one of the sponges and sandwiched the second on top. "Um, looks delicious! Anything I can sample?"

"No, there isn't!" Margaret replied firmly. "Clive will be in about eight. Until then you'll have to contain your soul in patience. I've the boys to feed and bath first."

"Cruel woman!" complained Nicholas, as he wiped a finger round the bowl Margaret had just been using. "Can't I have a slice with my nephews-to-be?"

Margaret stacked the mixing bowls and the other crockery in the sink, and quickly wiped the table and the working surfaces with a damp cloth. She opened the oven, and peeped in. The tarts were done, so she took them out and put them to cool.

"Now if you feel strong enough, and would like a job, you can help me bath the boys."

The next threequarters of an hour were the most hilarious Margaret ever remembered. Those people, even herself included, who thought of Nicholas as a hard, cynical man, should have seen him with the two little boys. Nothing was too silly for him to get up to, and the twins laughed until they could only sit exhaustedly on Margaret's knee, swathed in two large bath towels.

"Oh, Uncle Nick, do that funny duck again," they pleaded. But Margaret broke in at last, trying to make her voice severe.

"I might remind you I've all this mess to clear up before you get any tea, so that's enough for tonight," and she frowned up at Nicholas.

He leaned wearily against the bathroom wall, and wiped his damp forehead with the back of a hand. He was laughing himself as he looked down at her. As she glanced up, a twin held comfortably in each arm, Margaret could almost have imagined she saw tenderness in his eyes. She glanced away again quickly. He ought to have a family himself, she thought, not be playing with someone else's. And then the colour flooded her already hot cheeks as she thought that maybe that was the reason he was getting married. Maybe a family was the main object behind the odd marriage bargain he had proposed.

When the boys were in pyjamas and dressing gowns, they were given pickabacks down to the living-room. Margaret put one twin in each corner of the commodious settee, and handed Nicholas a story book.

"Over to you! I'm going to get their supper," and with a mischievous smile twitching the corner of her mouth, she went away leaving Nicholas standing looking quizzically after her.

When she returned with a laden trolley fifteen minutes later, it was to find her nephews snuggling cosily on either side of him, and Nicholas's deep, drawling voice putting magic into the story he was reading. He closed the book when he saw her and said, "The rest of the story afterwards. Come on, let's eat."

Despite wails of reluctance at being interrupted, Paul and Keith fell on the food with gusto. Margaret had made a pot of tea when she had prepared the nursery meal, and she poured Nicholas a cup and handed it to him, saying, "I think you've earned that."

As he watched the two small boys hungrily putting away the mound of sandwiches and cakes which Margaret had provided, Nicholas suddenly looked up over their heads and met her eyes. Margaret looked away quickly, hoping that he had not seen the wistful longing in her own eyes, and wishing for the hundredth time that she could read his expression.

She had thought to see tenderness earlier when they had been bathing the children. But was that only wishful thinking? And this present glance. Had it really held the sort of look she had seen Clive so often give her sister, or was it only a figment of her imagination? When she turned her head and glanced at him again, however, he had looked away and was busily wiping chocolate cake off Paul's face with a clean white handkerchief.

As she pushed the trolley into the kitchen, Margaret took herself to task. If you let your imagination run riot like this, she told herself severely, you'll be fancying Nicholas madly in love with you before very long. And you know that isn't so, my girl.

She was just drying the last of the crockery and preparing potatoes for the evening meal, when Nicholas walked back into the kitchen, a boy on each arm.

Margaret smiled over her shoulder. "They're too heavy. You'll give at the knees."

Nicholas eyed her, disgust in his look. "Too heavy! What nonsense you women talk sometimes. Are they to go up to bed now? And that reminds me, have you unpacked that basket I brought?"

"No. What's in it? I hope you haven't brought tons of food."

"No, but I raided the kitchen before I left home. Thought it might save you doing a lot of cooking. Shall I take the boys upstairs?"

Margaret nodded as she began to open the parcels in the basket. "Yes, please. See they brush their teeth before they get into bed, won't you? Oh, and it's Paul's week for the upper bunk. They take it in turns."

She went on unwrapping the parcels as she took them out of the basket. There was a jar of jellied soup. In a plastic covered bowl she found salad, already prepared for the table. Another wrapped parcel revealed steak, and at the bottom she discovered a pound of butter, cracker biscuits and a box of assorted cheeses.

Margaret whisked a duster over the dining-room, and quickly set the table. She prepared the steak and put potatoes on to begin cooking.

For several minutes she had been aware of giggles overhead which were getting louder. She ran upstairs and put her head round the door of the twins' bedroom. The boys were both sitting in their dressing gowns on the top bunk while Nicholas walked from wall to wall on his hands.

Margaret stood, just inside the door, and looked down. As he suddenly spotted her, he stood slowly upright. Her dimple was very much in evidence as she said, "I'd give anything for some of your starchier friends to see you now!"

Nicholas tucked in his shirt and ran his hands over his hair. Then he walked towards her and before Margaret could guess his intention, he had swung her up into his arms.

The boys gave renewed shrieks of delight as Margaret struggled and pleaded to be put down, while Nicholas, with the utmost ease, rocked her to and fro, ignoring her struggles.

"What shall I do to punish you for your rude remarks, my lady? What do you think you deserve?"

Margaret secretly thrilled at the strength she could feel in the arms holding her, but embarrassed and dishevelled by the skirmish, suddenly decided that discretion was the better part of valour. She disarmed him by looking pleadingly into his eyes and saying softly, "Please put me down."

Nicholas stood completely still for one long moment gazing back into her eyes, and Margaret's heart beat quicker as she wondered exactly what he was going to do next. But he surprised her yet again by swinging her up on to the top bunk, and sitting her there between the boys, her feet dangling well off the floor.

"Sit there a minute, girl dear, while I finish the exhibition," and Margaret found herself an unwilling addition to his audience while he completed a series of acrobatics for the twins' amusement.

At last, when even the excitable boys had had enough, Nicholas lifted her down, and they tucked two tired, happy little boys into their beds. As the sound of their baby prayers followed them down the stairs, Margaret was pained again by the thought of the might-have-been.

By the time Clive arrived home from his evening visit to see his wife and new baby son, the meal was almost ready. The steaks were grilling nicely and golden-brown potatoes were sautéing in a pan. If he was surprised to see his future brother-in-law looking so much at home, Clive made no comment and merely greeted Nicholas cheerfully.

When the supper had been eaten and cleared away, the two men helped Margaret to wash up, and then took two tankards of beer into the garden and sat in the warm summer evening, drinking and talking. Margaret found Jean's mending basket, and settled herself in an armchair, just inside the open french windows, and listened idly to the conversation outside. One thing about Nicholas Hollis—when he wished he could make himself agreeable to anyone, young or old, male or female. He was as much a success with Clive, as with

Aunt Mary or the boys. Why couldn't she just be content to accept him as he was without wishing for his love? This marriage could be a success if she didn't expect too much.

It was not until Nicholas had gone home that she remembered they had both been invited to a dinner party that evening. And yet he must have refused for them both, apparently preferring a quiet family evening rather than interesting conversation round his friends' dinner table.

The next day, the applicants for Margaret's position were interviewed. Mrs. Hollis quickly decided that one of them, a very pleasant, if rather prim-voiced, young lady would suit her. Margaret herself had been rather drawn to Pamela Purcell when the six applicants had sat in her office earlier. She was the only one of the six who had sat displaying no sign of nerves. The ideal person, thought Margaret, to deal with some of the "charitably" minded ladies who served on committees. She was therefore delighted when her employer told her that Miss Purcell would be coming to start learning the work on the following Monday.

All that week, Margaret hurried off at five o'clock to cope with her nephews. To her surprise, Nicholas turned up each evening, if not for a meal then in time to have a drink and talk before bedtime.

On the following Monday, Miss Purcell arrived. Margaret found that the prim voice, the care with which she pronounced each word, was a bit alarming to start with, but she was so obviously going to be pleasant and easy to get on with, and they were soon on christian name terms. When Margaret mentioned that her sister would be coming out of hospital with a new baby the following Thursday, it was Pamela Purcell herself who suggested that she could manage alone for one day if Margaret wanted to be on hand when her new nephew arrived home.

Nicholas, who had come in to have some letters

typed in the middle of this discussion, at once seconded Pamela's suggestion, and arranged to take the twins out during the morning while Margaret cleaned and cooked without interruption.

As a result, there was quite a reception committee waiting when Clive drove up to the house shortly after lunch, and assisted his wife to get out of the car. Not only Margaret, Nicholas and the boys were eagerly awaiting Jean and the baby, but Mrs. Willis too. The latter had arrived unexpectedly early that morning, a box of detergent in one hand, a scrubbing brush in the other. She had set to work alongside Margaret with a brief, "Thought I'd just come along and give you a hand with Miss Jean's place, Miss Margaret. Get it done in half the time, we will."

The scrap of humanity in Jean's arms was duly admired, hugged, kissed and finally put in his cot. The family began to sort itself out. Clive reluctantly had to leave to return to his office, but Nicholas stayed on to take Margaret home after the boys had been put early to bed.

"You get off now, darling, and thanks a million for all you've both done," Jean said as she shooed them off. "Go and see a film or something. You must be sick of the sight of children and a kitchen."

Nicholas grinned as he slid into his seat. "She little knows you enjoyed every moment of it," he said as he slipped the car into gear.

Margaret sat silent. How had he known? And had he, in his own uncanny manner, also detected how much she wished she had been doing it for a family of her own? She sincerely hoped not. The less he knew of her innermost thoughts and longings, the better. She was vulnerable enough, heaven knew, where he was concerned.

The next couple of weeks passed like lightning. Her days were spent initiating Miss Purcell in the intricasies of the job, her evenings with Nicholas, and at the week-end Margaret made her usual visit to see her mother. Mrs. Hollis too was beginning to urge her to start thinking about her wedding dress. She gave Margaret a book of bridal patterns one morning and told her to look through it, "For you can't expect Mrs. Krol to produce something really gorgeous in five minutes," she told her.

Margaret picked up the book reluctantly and leafed through it. "But I never thought of a white wedding with all the trimmings," she stammered. "I'd imagined we would be married somewhere very quietly."

Mrs. Hollis looked a little surprised at her words, but before they could continue the conversation, Mrs. Macgennis knocked to say that an unexpected caller had arrived.

Margaret was congratulating herself on having postponed the question of the wedding dress, but she discovered, a few hours later, that Mrs. Hollis must have tackled her son on the same subject. As he and Margaret were finishing dinner that night, for once dining alone together in a quiet restaurant, he broached the subject of the wedding date.

"I want to be back in Salisbury by the second week in August, so how about us deciding on August the second for the wedding? It won't be very long for you to get your things ready, so how about us getting that settled? Mother tells me you've done nothing yet *about* a wedding dress—and what about clearing your flat?"

He looked searchingly at Margaret's averted face.

"Are you going to let it furnished, or what? If you clear out your personal belongings, maybe Clive could attend to that after we're gone."

Margaret stared down at the ash tray before she replied.

"I've not given it much thought yet," she said at last, and was surprised when he replied, a glint of quick anger in his eyes, "Then it's about time you did."

Margaret looked quickly at him, and away again. "There's such a lot to be decided. What about Mother?

170

She won't want to miss the wedding, and yet how can she get to the church?"

Nicholas stubbed out his cigarette and said brusquely, "There's no reason why she shouldn't be wheeled into church in a chair, but we'd have to decide whether we'd have the wedding in Bournemouth or whether she should come and stay with your sister for a couple of days. We could of course get married without her and then drive down and see her before we leave England. I'd thought we might go back to Africa by easy stages. A couple of days in Rome, say, and then a week in Nairobi. You've not seen either, you tell me, and we can do some sightseeing if that appeals to you. However, it's for you to decide."

Margaret had to blink rapidly. It would never do to cry in front of Nicholas, still less in a crowded dining-room.

"May I discuss it with you again when I've had a chance to talk to Mother and Jean this week-end?" she asked, and then, as Nicholas nodded, she said hesitantly, "You're sure, aren't you, that you really want to marry me, Nick?"

She was not aware that she had used the boy's diminution of his name, as she smiled across the table at him.

Nicholas smiled slowly, the wickedly heart-catching smile which Margaret felt sure no woman could resist.

"Now that," he said, "is the stupidest thing you've said yet. Am I the sort of man to do anything I really don't wish to?"

He had answered her question with another, Margaret noticed. He turned away to speak to the waiter at that moment, and the conversation lapsed. Had it been intentional on his part?

Margaret pleaded tiredness that evening, and Nicholas ran her home early. A brief kiss, and he had gone. Margaret let herself into the flat, and wandered into the living-room. It was not yet quite dark, and the furniture stood out solidly black in the dusky room.

171

As she stood, lost in thought, looking out on to the quiet garden, the telephone rang behind her. Wondering who could be ringing at that time of night, Margaret lifted the receiver. It was the matron of the nursing home in Bournemouth.

Some instinct told Margaret this would not be good news.

"Miss Grant, I'm sorry to be the bearer of bad news, but I'm afraid you must brace youself for a shock." Margaret's hand tightened on the telephone, but she did not speak. The matron went on, "About half an hour after your mother settled down for the night, Sister went in to see if she was comfortable, and found she had slipped away quietly in her sleep. She was perfectly well during the day or I would have rung earlier and warned you. I'm sorry to give you a shock like this, but it was to be expected, you know."

As Margaret did not answer, the matron said quickly, "Are you still there, Miss Grant?"

Margaret licked dry lips and replied. "Yes, thank you, Matron. I understand. I'll come down first thing tomorrow. Is that all right? Or perhaps I should come tonight?"

"No, no, there's nothing you can do tonight. I'll see you in the morning, my dear. Good night! And I'm very sorry to have to ring you like this."

Margaret wished her good night and rang off. She stood for some minutes, her hand still on the receiver. It seemed impossible that her brave, cheerful, darling mother could have died. But at least she had suffered no pain. Then Margaret pulled herself together and, lifting the receiver, rang for a taxi.

When she got to her sister's house, she asked the taxi-driver to wait, and went quietly round to the back door. A light was burning in the kitchen and she tapped softly.

When Clive opened the door, he gave an exclamation of surprise.

"Sorry to come so late, Clive. I've had bad news and

didn't want to telephone in case it disturbed Jean or the baby."

"Jean isn't asleep," he replied, "I'm just making her a hot drink. What is it?"

Margaret told him briefly. "I've a taxi waiting. I've got to go down first thing tomorrow to the nursing home, and I think I'll go straight home now. You'll break it to Jean, won't you?"

"I've a better idea than that. Pay off the taxi and stay here the night. I'll take you down in the morning. You can't go and make all the arrangements alone."

Jean took the news badly, and Margaret and Clive had their work cut out calming her down and settling her off to sleep. She wanted to come too when they told her that they intended driving down to Bournemouth the following morning, but eventually Clive dissuaded her.

"Someone must stay with the baby and the boys, you know, darling, so wouldn't it be better if you left it to Margaret and me?" he asked her, and finally she agreed.

Margaret passed a disturbed night, still shocked at the sudden news, and worried about her sister. But to her relief, Jean was up the next morning before them all, and Margaret found her sister cooking breakfast and dealing with the boys' early morning high spirits quite calmly and without any trace of the tears of the preceding night. She made Margaret eat a proper breakfast before she left with Clive, and even offered to ring and tell Mrs. Hollis what had happened.

"Don't worry about me, Margaret. I'll not mope. It was just the shock, and I should so have liked Mother to see David before she . . . before she . . ." Jean turned away abruptly. Margaret gave her sister's shoulder a quick squeeze as she passed her to collect her coat.

When Clive and Margaret returned, late that evening, they found Nicholas sitting with Jean. They had a light supper, eating picnic fashion, while they discussed the happenings of the day.

It had been no easy one for Margaret. She had had a

harrowing half hour during the afternoon with Mrs. Salmon, and she was glad to sit quietly in her comfortable chair, picking at the food on her plate, and listening to Clive's voice outlining the arrangements they had made for the funeral.

When Nicholas rose to run Margaret home, she collected her things and went out to the car, secretly anticipating the moment when she would be alone to marshal her thoughts. She was surprised, therefore, out of her musings, to hear Nicholas say quietly, "It didn't occur to you, I suppose, to ring last night and put me in the picture?"

Margaret hesitated for a moment before she answered.

"Well, to be honest, it didn't. My only thought was of getting to Jean and breaking the news carefully. Women aren't at their best, you know, immediately after having a baby."

Her tones were faintly pleading. Despite his calm tones, she guessed Nicholas was annoyed. The silence stretched between them after she finished speaking. After several minutes she went on. "Clive did all that was necessarry, you know. It wasn't as if you could have done anything. I'm sorry I didn't tell you, Nicholas, but the news was such a shock, late at night—I was unprepared, wasn't expecting . . ." Her voice trailed away as the tears rose, choking her. She swallowed them back with an effort.

"Sorry," Nicholas's voice was abrupt, not his usual soft, easy drawl, "that was unforgivable of me. You're upset enough, I know. Forget I said it." He gave a bark of laughter, completely lacking in amusement. He handed her his handerchief. "Here, blow!"

Margaret blew her nose, realizing that she wasn't going to have those quiet minutes to think things out. The important thing now, she thought, was to get it over, to say what had been niggling at the back of her mind all through the ordeal of the day. In the midst of her grief the one thought that had been with her was that she couldn't hold Nicholas now, it wouldn't be fair.

"I wanted to talk to you, Nicholas. Now Mother is dead, there's no need——" She stopped uneasily, aware of the electricity in the atmosphere, not knowing how to go on. She had been about to say that he must not feel bound to her now the main reason for their bargain was gone.

Nicholas pulled up outside her flat. As he turned to face her she realized she had never seen him so angry. "I've been waiting for something like this ever since Mother told me the news this morning," he began. "I suppose you intended coming to me in the morning and telling me prettily that here was my ring and a cheque to cover my expenditure and inconvenience. There's a word to describe people who don't keep to an agreement. A very rude word. Did you know?"

Margaret was trembling too much to answer. She had never thought he would react like this, had felt that now her mother was dead it behoved her at least to offer him his freedom, reluctant though she was to do so. She had never properly understood his real reasons for offering to help her in the first place, and as little did she understand this unreasonable anger when she now tried to set him free.

She was still trying to think of how she could answer him when Nicholas spoke again. "We'll say no more about it, then." He had obviously got the wild flare of anger under control. "I didn't intend to blow up like that and add to your problems. I really am most sincerely sorry about your mother. Now I suggest you go in and get to bed," and he got out to come round and help her out of the car.

Margaret did not return to work until after the funeral. Miss Purcell was by now well able to cope without her. When she did eventually return, she found herself handing more and more of the work over to Pamela's capable hands.

Now that a date had been decided, preparations for the wedding were going ahead. To Margaret's relief, because of her mother's death, these were to be on a much quieter and smaller scale than Mrs. Hollis had originally planned. The wedding invitations had been sent out to only very close relatives and friends, but already presents were beginning to arrive in what, to Margaret, seemed to be ever-increasing numbers.

Afterwards, Margaret had no clear recollection of those days. She seemed to spend them suspended in a soap bubble, a bubble which could so easily burst. Though Nicholas had never once referred to their conversation in the car, the relaxed, easy way in which he had treated her in those weeks immediately prior to her mother's death had vanished as if they had never been. He was always polite, always attentive, but nowadays he kept her at a distance. Sometimes, when he had left her in the evenings, Margaret let herself into the flat and sat in her darkened room turning things dismally over in her mind.

It was almost with a sense of inevitability therefore that she heard Blanche Miln-Prescott's voice on the telephone one morning. At the effusive note in Blanche's voice, Margaret became instantly wary, "Is that Miss Grant speaking? It is! Good! Blanche Miln-Prescott here. Now look, Margaret—I may call you that, mayn't I?" Without waiting for an answer she continued, "I wonder if you'd care to come and have lunch with Mother and me today. I know it's very short notice, but we've had several things sent on approval and we can't decide which to choose for your present. Will you come and tell us which you'd prefer? Do say 'yes'. Come early, then we can have a nice long talk."

Margaret hesitated for a moment. "But wouldn't it be better for Nicholas to come too? Perhaps we might pop in for a drink this evening. I really would perfer him to come and see the presents with me. It's very kind of you both to take all this trouble."

Margaret felt a hypocrite. As she spoke, a part of her

176

mind remembered all the past snubs which the Miln-Prescotts had administered when they regarded her merely as one of the Hollis's paid employees. She recalled too the words she had overheard the day her engagement to Nicholas had been announced. It was strange that Blanche should bother to be so agreeable to someone she had described not many weeks ago as "a little ninny, just like Julie".

But before she could muster more excuses, the voice spoke in her ear again. "Oh, nonsense! Nicholas would want you to do the choosing. That's settled, then. Twelve-thirty," and before Margaret could speak again, she was cut off.

When she rang the bell of the Miln-Prescotts' flat on the dot of twelve-thirty, Margaret again felt apprehension creeping over her. However, nothing could have been more gracious that the welcome she received when Blanche opened the door a minute later.

When she was comfortably settled in a chair in the spacious sitting-room, Blanche sat down herself and leaned back. "We're so glad you could come. Mother is just supervising the lunch. "Ah, there you are, Mother!" as Mrs. Miln-Prescott hurried into the room and shook hands with Margaret. "I was just saying how pleased we were that Margaret could come."

Mrs. Miln-Prescott glanced across at her daughter before she nodded. "Oh yes, of course. Now, Miss Grant —I mean, Margaret. Before we go into lunch, Blanche and I would like you to tell us which of these you would prefer," and she went over to a side table on which Margaret could see several parcels.

As they were unwrapped for her inspection, Margaret wondered whether she should stall until Nicholas could see them, but then an inner voice hinted that, in any case, he wouldn't be very interested. So far, he had paid little attention to the presents now arriving almost daily, so with suitable thanks and admiration for their choice, Margaret selected a piece of display china from the gifts which had been laid out for her approval.

By the time lunch was served and they had gone into the dining-room, Margaret had nearly run out of polite conversation. She managed to keep going through lunch and was congratulating herself on brushing through a very awkward hour fairly creditably, when Blanche suddenly asked her if she had to be back by two o'clock.

"Is it that already? I really must go, then," Margaret answered as she glanced at her watch.

"Perhaps you'd like to tidy up before you leave," Blanche suggested. "Come along to my room."

Margaret followed, wondering whether the choice of words had been deliberate and already feeling that she must have sat through lunch with a smut on her nose or her lipstick smudged. A quick glance in the mirror of the bathroom which led off Blanche's bedroom reassured her.

When she emerged, Blanche was sitting on the bed smoking a cigarette. As Margaret put her handbag on the dressing table, she could not help noticing the two photographs in large silver frames, which stood side by side.

One was a studio portrait in colour, and Margaret might have been looking at a photograph of her younger self. The girl in the hyacinth-blue dress had hair more auburn than Margaret's, but the shape of the face, the sweetness of the mouth, and the willowy figure were Margaret's to the life. If a closer scrutiny might have shown a weakness of the chin and a lack of the character which showed so clearly in Margaret's own face, she did not notice.

The other photograph was obviously the enlargement of a holiday snap. A young man looking down lovingly at the girl in his arms. A younger, handsomer, happier Nicholas, with none of the lines in his forehead and down the sides of his mouth.

As Margaret's trembling hands dealt with powder compact and comb, Blanche's silky voice sounded from behind her. "The very image of you, isn't she? That was my sister, you know. The moment Nicholas

178

set eyes on you, I knew he'd try to get you to fill Julie's shoes. He's never really got over losing her, you know."

Margaret shut her handbag before replying.

"No, I didn't know." She turned resolutely to the figure on the bed. "As a matter of fact, Nicholas rarely mentions your sister, and he's never given me the impression of a man still worshipping a dead ideal."

She forced a mocking smile to her lips. "People do fall for similar tpyes, I'm told. Men who prefer blondes don't usually end up marrying brunettes, you know."

Blanche got up quickly and stubbed out her cigarette. She looked coldly at Margaret, all pretence of pleasantness at an end.

"Well, we all have our own ideas of why Nicholas asked you to marry him, of course. That night you spent down at Lyndhurst probably had something to do with it."

"The night we spent . . ." Margaret stopped. "But I'm afraid I don't understand."

"Don't you? That naïve act doesn't cut any ice with me, Miss Grant. A close friend of Mother's saw Nicholas Hollis come out of your bedroom at an unusually late hour. Unfortunate, wasn't it, that she too spent a few days at that particular hotel?"

"When we had that breakdown and had to stay the night, Nicholas and I were already engaged," Margaret said. "But in any case, I'm sure Nicholas doesn't know and wouldn't care what any of your friends may have thought."

"Wouldn't you? Ah, but then it's possible Nicholas has been brought up to have different moral standards." Margaret clenched her teeth, it was as much as she could do not to strike the arrogant face in front of her. Blanche continued, "Even if Nicholas has regretted his hasty engagement, he couldn't possibly cry off now. But of course that's something you wouldn't understand."

Despite her anger and the sick feeling this scene was giving her, Margaret couldn't help laughing. She picked up her handbag and turned to the door. "Really, Miss

Miln-Prescott, aren't you being a bit novelettish? I don't know what your motive was for inviting me here and then being so very unpleasant, but I think it would be better if we both forgot this conversation ever took place. Thank you for the present. Now, if you'll excuse me I'll just say good-bye to your mother. I must go, I'm late as it is."

When Margaret walked to the lift, her knees were shaking under her. The sick feeling got worse instead of better, and when she came out of the block flats she turned in the direction of the park to give herself time to pull herself together.

She sat for ten minutes on a bench thinking over the events of the last hour. In her mind's eye, she saw the two photographs, and much she had not understood fell into place.

The speculation she had seen not only in Nannie Macgennis's eyes but in those of Mrs. Hollis when they knew Nicholas was on his way home. The surprise she had seen in his own eyes when he had greeted her that first day. It must have been a shock for him to see her in his own home, a living girl who might have been the twin of his dead wife.

No wonder, if he was thinking it was time he married and settled down, that he had picked on herself. Paddy-the-next-best-thing is what I should have been called, Margaret thought, smiling wryly to herself. But the next best thing isn't good enough for me. Now that I don't have to do it for Mother, can I really go on and marry a man who doesn't love me?

CHAPTER TEN

NICHOLAS was taking her to the ballet that night, and as Margaret pulled the short black evening gown, the bodice cut to resemble petals, over her head, she wished wholeheartedly that she was going home instead to have time to think things out properly in private. When she had arrived back that afternoon, it had been to find a lot of work had accumulated during her absence, and it had taken the combined efforts of herself and Pamela Purcell to get it all cleared away by the end of the day.

As they drove to the theatre, Nicholas himself did not seem to be in the sunniest of moods. After he had snubbed two or three of her remarks, Margaret relapsed into silence, but this only seemed to make him more disagreeable.

He remained like this until the end of the performance, his obvious inattention and restlessness communicating itself to Margaret, and making her lose half her own enjoyment in the grace of the dancing.

As he helped her into her coat, Nicholas caught the look of apprehension Margaret was giving him, and he suddenly smiled. When they turned to edge their way out of the row of seats, he pinched her elbow. "Sorry to be such a bear," he whispered in her ear. "I've had a hell of a day, but I shouldn't be taking it out on you."

As Margaret looked over her shoulder he asked, "Will you forgive me?"

Margaret smiled back and nodded. During the meal that followed, he laughed and talked and made an obvious effort to erase the memory of his earlier black mood. Margaret played up and did her share to make the evening enjoyable, but she longed to ask Nicholas to tell her what had put him in such a temper, and her inability to speak frankly only made her own spirits sink lower. Was he regetting his proposed marriage? Looking back, she knew he had not been his usual self since definite plans for their wedding had been made and the acceptances began to arrive. Was he perhaps remembering his first wedding day? Had Blanche been right in saying that he regretted his engagement and would have liked to back out of their bargain? But if that were the case, why had he been so angry and repudiated her attempts to break off? Perhaps it was a matter of pride. Perhaps not only for his own sake but to save wounding her own pride he had decided that they must go ahead with the wedding. But it did not seem to Margaret that he displayed any of the signs of a contented bridegroom. Quite the reverse.

It was a long time before she got to sleep that night, and when she did so, Margaret was troubled by uneasy dreams. In the end, she got up early and made herself a cup of tea. She sat at the kitchen table and on scraps of paper tried to work out the extent to which she was financially indebted to Nicholas. It came to quite a high total, and she spent the time before leaving for town trying to assess ways of raising this sum should she decide to ask Nicholas to release her from their engagement.

Margaret was still feeling in an unsettled state of mind when she arrived at the Hollises'. It did nothing to soothe her disturbed spirits to find that there was a committee meeting arranged for that morning.

It proved to be a long and difficult one, and did not finish until nearly lunchtime. The only bright spot was the exchange which Margaret overheard between Miss Purcell and Blanche Miln-Prescott. The latter had tried in her usual high-handed way to make Pamela Purcell feel small, but Pamela was of a different temperament from Margaret, and the conversation which she overheard as she hurried down to the office made her smile.

In her prim, precise tones, Miss Purcell was putting the overbearing snobbery of Blanche firmly in its place with one or two well-chosen words. Margaret could not help wondering what the outcome would be, but having got to know Pamela well during the short time they had been working together, Margaret thought that perhaps the odds were not this time on Blanche getting the best of the bout.

During the course of the next few days, Margaret found herself watching every move Nicholas made, and diagnosing his every word. Despite common sense telling her that Blanche had only been trying to stir up more mischief, in the light of the evidence of those two photographs, she became more and more uncertain of her ability to make a success of this abnormal marriage, yet more determined than ever not to let Nicholas realize her true feelings towards him.

In the end, it was a small thing which finally decided her. The proverbial straw which will break the camel's back.

They had been spending the evening with Jean and her family. Nicholas was lying on the lawn, a twin on his stomach and the other on his bent knees, when Jean, who was sitting in a deck-chair, said, "You know, you should have a gang of boys of your own, Nicholas."

Margaret caught the swift reply. "That's what I think myself." And with a grin in Margaret's direction, he added, "Believe me, I can't wait!"

Margaret got up quietly from where she had been sitting and went into the house. Though he had to all intents been funning she felt he had spoken with all seriousness. So she had been right in her thinking on one point at least. Nicholas had reached the age when he thought it time to settle down, and her likeness to Julie had probably clinched matters. Love just didn't enter into it as far as he was concerned. He'd done with that, but he did want children of his own.

When he left her that night, Margaret sat down and tried to write Nicholas a letter. After three attempts she gave it up and went to bed, her reasoning too disturbed to allow for straight thinking. But in the early hours of the morning, she awoke, her mind crystal clear, the words in which she would terminate their engagement and tactfully arrange repayment of the money he had disbursed for her mother clear-cut in her mind.

Before she could fall asleep again, she got up and wrote her letter, slipping in the beautiful emerald ring at the last minute before she sealed the envelope.

That evening, before she left the house, Margaret slipped into Nicholas's bedroom and stood the letter up on his dressing table. He was dining out with Miles that evening, she knew, so he would not be surprised that she had gone home without seeing him.

Margaret went straight home to the flat and had a meal, then, unable to sit still, she went to a cinema. She did not arrive home again until eleven o'clock, but no one came and the telephone remained silent.

So it did all through that interminable Saturday. To give herself something to do, Margaret cleaned the flat from top to bottom, hoping that it would make her too tired to think.

By lunchtime, the place was spotless, but Margaret's thoughts were still churning round relentlessly in her head. Perhaps Nicholas hadn't read the letter. Perhaps he'd had an accident. Unlikely, for she would have heard. Then after all he was going to take her at her word, and she would hear nothing more from him at all. But in that case, what was going to happen on Monday? Despite the fact that Miss Purcell would be there, Mrs. Hollis would expect her to arrive as usual for work.

During the afternoon, Margaret shopped, afterwards returning home to make a batch of the twins' favourite cakes. She took them over to her sister's house in time for the boys' tea.

On her arrival, it did not make Margaret feel any more cheerful to discover that Jean and Clive had arranged for a baby-sitter and were getting ready to dine out with one of Clive's clients.

"You should have rung and asked me to come and sit in," Margaret said, as she helped her sister to feed and bath the children. "I'd have come like a shot, you know that. There was no need to get in someone you'd have to pay."

Jean laughed. "Economical Margaret! Well, Mrs. Moore doesn't exactly come for halfpennies, but the children like her, and in any case Clive and I feel Nicholas will have something to say if we commandeer you every time we feel like an evening out together. Let's face it, darling, things aren't the same now you have a fiancé to consider. You did more than your share when wee David was born. You've no idea the relief it was to hear you'd taken over when I was rushed off like that."

Margaret picked up one of the twins and hid her hot face in his warm, sweet-smelling hair. I shall have to tell Jean, she thought, but not tonight. No, I can't tell her tonight. She blinked the tears determinedly from her eyes and plunged into a last game with the boys before they were popped into their bunk beds.

When the baby-sitter arrived, Margaret said good night and left. Not wanting to go home again to the empty flat and her unhappy thoughts, she went to see yet another film. It was a relief to get into the darkened cinema and stop pretending. She sat through three hours of news, cartoon and main feature without the slightest idea of what was happening on the screen.

Next morning, Margaret woke out of her broken sleep about six-thirty and lay listening to the birds singing outside her window. The sun was already coming up, and it promised to be a glorious summer day. She felt too tired after two nights with little sleep, and that interspersed with unhappy dreams, to appreciate either the sunshine or the birdsong in the garden. She got up unrefreshed and went slowly into the kitchen, switching on the immersion heater as she passed it.

When the kettle had boiled, Margaret took a cup of

tea back to the bedroom. She lay on top of the bed, almost too numbed by this time to collect her thoughts coherently. She put the cup down when it was empty and lay back, her eyes on the ceiling. Twenty-seven next week, she thought, and what have I to show for it? But the cracks on the ceiling offered her no answer. After a while she got up and trailed listlessly into the bathroom.

She had a hot bath, and then lay and let the cold water beat over her. When she had towelled herself briskly, she put on clean pants and bra and then pulled on navy blue slacks and a thick sweater. She found walking shoes and let herself out of the house.

She walked for over an hour. The streets were quiet, empty, the closed blinds and curtains showing where people were taking the opportunity to have a long, lazy Sunday morning. Only in one or two houses were children already playing in the gardens. The piping voices rising on the still summer air made Margaret smile. She remembered many happy mornings when she and Jean as youngsters had left their parents sleeping and crept down quietly to play during those long-ago summer holidays. What a happy childhood they had had.

The exercise, the beautiful morning all had their effect on her, and when Margaret finally returned home, she felt much better and her head clearer. When she got into the flat, she made her bed and threw the windows wide. In the kitchen she spread a gay checked cloth on the table and started cutting into a grapefruit. She had just put on the coffee when the front door bell rang. It kept on ringing as she quickly washed and dried her hands, and when she went down the hall and opened the front door, she understood why.

Nicholas was leaning against the wall beside the front door and had his finger firmly pressed against the bell push. As he heard the door open he looked up, and Margaret's heart sank.

On his face was the old look of bored indifference which had so antagonized her when she had first made his acquaintance. But now, instead of rousing her spirit as it had done then, it only induced in her a burning desire to weep.

He took his finger off the bell and straightened up. His disinterested glance passed over her slowly and almost insolently before he spoke.

"Had breakfast yet?"

Margaret still hadn't found her voice; she could only shake her head. Nicholas walked up the steps and with a brief "excuse me" he walked past into the hall. By the time Margaret had closed the door and turned round, he was walking down the hall to the kitchen. He pulled off his jacket as he did so, and threw it on to the nearest chair.

"Ah, good," he said as he rolled up the sleeves of his shirt, grapefruit! I'll have some. And cereals, please. Now, have you any bacon?" and before Margaret could answer, he had thrown open the door of the refrigerator and was examining the contents.

Nicholas took out bacon and a couple of eggs and lifted down the frying pan from its place on the kitchen wall. As he laid rashers of bacon in the pan, he remarked, "Do you want bacon, Meg?"

At the sound of the now familiar nickname, Margaret found her voice. "No, thank you. I'll just have toast."

"Then if you're going to do the toast, make enough for two, will you?"

Margaret cut bread, and plugged in the toaster. She laid another place, and put the grapefruit, now cut and sugared, on to the table. When the toast was done, she put the coffee and hot milk under cosies, and sat waiting for Nicholas to finish frying his eggs and bacon.

When these were cooked to his satisfaction, he put them on a plate to keep warm, and sitting down opposite Margaret, applied himself to the grapefruit. Most of the time he kept up a steady flow of easy conversation, very little of which required an answer.

Margaret followed his lead, answering him in a quiet

voice when this was necessary, and passing the sugar and condiments when required. She found she herself had no appetite, but ate her grapefruit and then took a piece of toast, and buttered it.

She was still nibbling at this when Nicholas pushed away his plate and took out his cigarette case. He asked her permission to smoke, and then for a moment sat silent, his eyes on the cigarettes as he carefully selected one.

When it was lighted and going to his satisfaction, he put his hand into his pocket again and taking something out, threw it on to the table between them.

"Before we go any further," he commanded, "put that on."

Margaret glanced down at her engagement ring winking from the cloth, then slowly she looked up into his face. Through the faint film of blue smoke his eyes looked into hers, demanding, mastering.

As she still made no movement, he picked up the ring and lifting her left hand, thrust the ring on to the third finger.

"That stays there until I change it for another," he said as his fingers left hers. "Or do you imagine that having carried out my side of the bargain, you're absolved by your mother's death from carrying out yours? I thought we'd sorted that one out a couple of weeks or so ago."

Margaret's face quivered slightly as the harsh words were barked out at her. Nicholas had put his cigarette case and lighter on the table, and hardly realizing what she was doing, Margaret reached out and took a cigarette.

She lighted it before she answered. Nicholas waited, his eyes on her face.

"I thought I explained that in my letter. Surely you understood?" Her voice was unconsciously appealing.

It fell on deaf ears.

"Explain! I know that you proposed—wasn't the word 'to reimburse' me? However, it's not money I want. It's a wife. Who do you suggest can fill that position if you don't? Have you any likely candidates in mind? Blanche perhaps?"

Margaret looked up sharply as the name was flung at her.

"Oh yes, I can guess she's had a hand in the making of this particular pie. What exactly had she been saying to you?"

The colour washed into Margaret's face in a hot tide, and Nicholas tilted his chair back and watched with malicious satisfaction.

"Hit the nail right on the head there, didn't I?" he remarked. "Well, you may as well tell me what poison she has put down this time, because if you don't, I shall ask Blanche myself."

Margaret stubbed out the half-smoked cigarette. Then she looked up and straightened in her chair as she met the mocking smile in his eyes.

She said slowly, "It wasn't so much what Blanche said, as the culmination of a great many things. You felt sorry for Mother and me, I think, in the first place. And then I'd always wondered what you saw in me. When Blanche told me that I was the image of your first wife, a lot of little things fell into place. Remarks Mrs. Macgennis made before you came home. A sort of speculation your mother has shown from time to time. I had vaguely wondered why they were all curious to see your reaction to meeting me. It wasn't until Thursday, when Blanche showed me your wife's photograph, that I understood. But it's no good, Nicholas. I can't compete with a ghost even if you felt anything more for me than pity. Perhaps the fact that I needed financial help tipped the scales. Added to that, I realized at Jean's the other evening that you had got to the age when settling down with a wife and family appealed to the patriach in you. I'm sorry, but I find I can't marry you after all on those terms."

"Been doing a good deal of thinking, haven't you, my dear?" Nicholas remarked dryly when she finally fell silent. "Well, let's take things one at a time. Granted, you are a little like Julie. And when I say a little, I mean a little. You're about the same height and size, the hair colouring is almost identical, but there the likeness ends, despite the evidence of the photograph.

"Julie, my love, hadn't your character, nor your spirit. From childhood, she had been crushed by two females determined that she should remain either completely in the background or come a very poor third in that household. I loved her very much, but the love I felt was three-quarters pity and a quarter the affection one feels for any sweet girl one has known all one's life. I know that now. I was only twenty-one when we married, and I'd great ideas, I suppose, of saving her from overwhelming odds, like some knight of old."

Nicholas stopped speaking, and smiled ironically.

"Young as I was, it didn't take me long to realize that even marriage wasn't going to save Julie. Quite the reverse. It woke in Blanche a greater demon of jealousy than ever before, and since I was away in the Air Force, she had a free hand to interfere between us.

"When Julie was killed, it was because Blanche had driven her nearly out of her mind telling her some story that I was interested in another woman. Julie wrote me a long, almost hysterical letter, posted it, and then decided after all to drive down to the base and have it out with me face to face. She was killed on that journey down. I received her letter two days later. It had been sent on by my Commanding Officer after I had gone home for the funeral."

Nicholas stopped speaking and took out another cigarette. Margaret noticed that his hands were not absolutely steady. She licked her lips and had started to frame a reply, when he spoke again.

"I tackled Blanche, of course, but she denied everything. Said Julie was unstable and it was just the imaginations of an hysterical girl. I didn't take any further action then, but I warned her when you and I became engaged. I knew she would make mischief again if she could."

"Maybe she does want to marry you herself," Margaret interrupted quietly.

Nicholas laughed. It was an ugly laugh, completely without mirth. "Well, she's doing her best to see I don't have any married life at all. I got off to a bad start with you, but events fell my way, and I thought everything was going to turn out well. Then your mother died and immediately you tried to break things off. That put paid to my high hopes at last of having a happy home of my own, with a loved and loving wife at the centre of it. I was a fool."

Nicholas rose abruptly and walked to the window. He stood there, his back to her. Margaret waited a moment to see if he had anything more to say, and when he neither turned nor spoke, she pushed her chair aside from the table and faced towards him.

"It seems we've both misunderstood each other, Nicholas," she said quietly. "I didn't know any of this. In fact, all these weeks, I thought I was being used as a sort of makeshift."

As he turned, hands in pockets, he said, "Makeshift? Makeshift what?"

Margaret smiled wistfully at him.

"Makeshift wife. I thought that after deciding you'd like a wife and family, you looked around for one who wouldn't interfere too much; who would be happy to remain in the background, and that the fact I was the double of Julie and also really did desperately need financial help, prompted you to ask me to marry you. You were always courteous and kind, I know, but I thought that was just good manners."

Nicholas smiled, with real amusement this time.

"And the kisses? Just momentary desire?"

Margaret's colour deepened, but she faced him bravely.

"Well, let's face it! Men will be men; they haven't sawdust in their veins."

Nicholas stood by the window, his hands still in his pockets, and held her glance.

"And now?" he asked.

Margaret could not look away; she could not answer. She had the impression he was willing her to do something, say something. He said again, "And now, Meg? What do you think now?"

Margaret's eyes looked steadily at him, at the lean, virile strength, the lazy grace of the whipcord figure, hands in pockets still. Looked at the muscular forearms displayed by the rolled shirt sleeves, the crisp, short haircut, the grey eyes. Yes, those grey eyes were smiling at her, though his mouth remained in a serious line. Those grey eyes were willing her to make the first move, and against her will, despite her pride, she did so.

She got up slowly and walked across to stand in front of him.

Margaret put up her hands and held his face between them. She said softly, "And now, Nicholas, I think we've talked enough. Too much, in fact. I just want to kiss you," and she did so.

When she took her mouth from his, Nicholas still stood with his hands in his pockets, but the smile in his eyes had reached his lips. He remained perfectly motionless for the space of a minute, just looking at her. Margaret got the impression that he was savouring the moment, delighting in the pleasure of just gazing at her. Then he gave a long sigh, removed his hands from his pockets, and reached out his arms for her.

"How right you are, my sweet Meg," he said. "We've talked enough. I, too, just want to kiss you."

Which he did. Very thoroughly. And Margaret discovered she hadn't sawdust in her veins either.

THE END